P9-DHN-451

The VOTING BOOTH

The VOTING BOOTH

BRANDY COLBERT

HYPERION

Los Angeles New York

First Edition, July 2020
1 3 5 7 9 10 8 6 4 2
FAC-020093-20143

Printed in the United States of America

This book is set in Officina and Sabon/Monotype; Canvas/Yellow Design Studio/Fontspring; KG Life is Messy/Kimberley Geswein Fonts/Fontspring.
Designed by Marci Senders

Library of Congress Cataloging-in-Publication Data
Names: Colbert, Brandy, author.
Title: The voting booth / Brandy Colbert.
Description: First edition. • Los Angeles : Disney-Hyperion, 2020. • Audience: Ages 12–18. • Audience: Grades 7–9. • Summary: The first year they are eligible to vote, Marva and Duke meet at their polling place and, over the course of one crazy day, fall in love.
Identifiers: LCCN 2019054677 (print) • LCCN 2019054678 (ebook) • ISBN 9781368053297 (hardcover) • ISBN 9781368053686 (ebook)
Subjects: CYAC: Politics, Practical—Fiction. • Love—Fiction. • African Americans—Fiction.
Classification: LCC PZ7.C66998 Vot 2020 (print) • LCC PZ7.C66998 (ebook) • DDC [Fic]—dc23
LC record available at https://lccn.loc.gov/2019054677
LC ebook record available at https://lccn.loc.gov/2019054678

Reinforced binding

Visit www.hyperionteens.com

Logo Applies to Text Stock Only

FOR MY HERO,
FANNIE LOU HAMER

The VOTING BOOTH

MARVA

I DON'T LIKE IT WHEN PEOPLE MAKE HYPERBOLIC statements, so I really mean it when I say I've been waiting for this day my entire life.

November 3. Election Day. But not just any election day—it's the first one that I'll be able to vote in. *Finally.*

I'm still doing my morning stretches when there's a knock at my door.

"Come in." I bring my right knee up to my chest to stretch my lower back. At the foot of my bed, my Maine

Coon, Selma, does her own kitty stretches, flexing her furry paws.

"Morning, sweetie." My mother is standing in the doorway of my bedroom, holding her NURSES CALL THE SHOTS coffee mug. "Just wanted to make sure you didn't oversleep for the big day."

"Mom." I peer around my knee to give her a look. "When was the last time I overslept?"

She takes a sip of coffee, thinking, then shrugs. "Never, I guess. You even showed up two weeks before your due date."

"Early is on time and on time is late," I say, pulling up my other knee. "That goes for babies, too."

Mom shakes her head, but she's smiling. "Is Alec going with you to the polling place?"

My leg falls back to the bed. "I'm not currently speaking to Alec." Well, he doesn't know that—but that doesn't make it any less true.

"What in the world did Mr. Perfect do to make you so mad?"

I wish she didn't look so amused. I hate it when adults do that—act like what we're going through isn't serious just because we're younger than them. She *knows* I hate that, and I can tell she's trying to swallow her smile, but it's not working. And it just makes a fresh wave of anger roll through me.

I sit up, lace my fingers together, and bend at the waist, stretching my arms over my head. "He's not voting."

That makes the smile drop. "*Your* Alec?" She pauses. "Isn't voting?"

"He says it doesn't make a difference. That the two-party system is antiquated and useless."

He's said more than that over the past couple of days, but I truly thought he'd change his mind. We've been together for almost two and a half years, since we were sophomores. I know him better than anyone. I also know that he can be stubborn, and that I can usually sway him in the most stubborn of moments. Not this time.

"But he's been canvassing with you." Mom frowns, straightening the top of her scrubs.

"And text-banking and visiting senior centers to get people registered," I add, shifting my stretch to the other side. Selma looks at me and yawns.

Alec was all in—or at least I thought he was. I glance at my phone on the nightstand, thinking of the last text he sent before I went to sleep last night:

I've thought about this, and you're not going to change my mind, Marv. It's my choice, not yours.

I didn't respond.

"Well, the polls are open until seven. He still has time to come to his senses."

I'm not holding my breath. Besides, things have been weird with Alec since we had the big college talk a couple of weeks ago. I'm not sure what's going on with us, but I need to set it aside for now. I've been waiting for this day forever.

Okay, so that was a little hyperbolic. But I *have* been interested in politics since I was a little girl. My second-grade teacher asked us to write down three things we wanted to be when we grew up. My choices were secretary of state, environmental attorney, and Supreme Court justice. Honestly, I'm pretty impressed with seven-year-old me for already knowing what she wanted.

"I'd better get out of here." Mom slugs the rest of her coffee, then swiftly crosses the room to give me a kiss. "Have a good day, sweetie. Try not to let Alec's civic irresponsibility wreck this for you."

Selma meows, looking right at my mother with her big hazel eyes.

"You have a good day, too, Selma," Mom says, scratching her soft little head before she leaves.

I finish stretching, untie my satin sleep scarf, and swing my legs over the side of the bed. Mom is right. I can't let Alec mess up this day for me.

It's way too important for that.

DUKE

"CUTTING IT A LITTLE CLOSE THIS MORNING, aren't you?"

"Forgot I had to get up early today," I say, leaning in to kiss Ma's cheek as she cracks eggs into a bowl.

Ma turns around, abandoning the eggs. "Duke Benjamin Crenshaw. Are you joking?"

"Yup," I say quickly, turning away to pour a glass of OJ so I don't have to look at her face. "Like I could forget today."

It's Election Day, and there are no jokes when it comes to politics in my house. Just nonstop talk about candidates and policies and campaigns. For real, every year feels like election year around here. And I know what Ma is thinking but won't say to me: *What would your brother think? This is no laughing matter.*

Julian died two years ago, but his name seems to always be on the tip of my mom's tongue. Ready to remind me of all the ways I'm not like him. All the ways I'm failing to honor his memory.

My little sis, Ida, stumbles into the kitchen, rubbing her eyes.

I snicker.

"What?" She shoots me a dirty look through her sleepy gaze as she plops down into her seat at the table.

"Wearing your sleep cap to school?"

She touches her head and groans. "It's too *early*. Why can't you go vote and come back for me? Or maybe Dana and her dad can swing by and get me?"

The skillet clatters on the stove.

"Absolutely not!"

Damn. I really don't want to see Ma's face now.

I slide a glass of juice in front of Ida and pop some bread in the toaster. Just in case. Ma might revolt and decide not to make us breakfast if we keep this up, and I need something stronger than cereal for today.

"You may be too young to vote, but you can still come along and see what it's all about," she says to Ida. "You're never too young for democracy."

"I know," Ida grumbles. I'm impressed she doesn't remind Ma that we both went with her and Dad to vote in the last presidential election, but I think she knows not to push it.

Ma scrambles her famous cheesy eggs silently for a couple of minutes, then puts two plates in front of us. I bring over the toast and the butter dish. We sit down at the same time.

"Listen," Ma says with a sigh. She pushes a hand through her short blond hair. "I know you could never forget how important this is, but you have to remember, these candidates are going to shape policies for years. And so many of the issues on the ballot and in their campaigns were important to Julian—gun violence in particular, but there's also immigration reform, prison reform.... So much is at stake. He would be so disappointed if he knew you weren't taking this seriously."

Both Ida and I drop our eyes to our laps. But Ma doesn't let us off the hook that easily.

"Duke."

I look up at her.

"He used to go over calendars with you and show you the date you'd be able to vote. He was so excited for you to turn eighteen." She looks at my sister. "And, Ida, I know you weren't around when Julian first got involved in our old community, but he came so far and—well, I guess I'll never stop wondering what he could have accomplished."

"Sorry, Ma," I say, staring at the eggs. I *love* those eggs, but I don't feel much like eating now. I remember looking at those calendars with Julian.

Can't wait till you can get in that voting booth, little homie. We gonna change lives. We gonna change the world.

"You're good kids," Ma says, squeezing my shoulder. She reaches across the table for Ida's hand. "You can't ever forget how important your voices are."

We wouldn't be having this talk if Dad were here. He doesn't like to mention Julian. Not like Ma does. If I wasn't related to him I might not even know he had a dead son.

We eat our breakfast listening to NPR's *Morning Edition*, unable to escape politics for even a second. Dude is blabbing about the assholes around the country trying to stop people from voting and how a lot of them are getting away with it. Ma is back up and at the sink, scrubbing the hell out of the egg pan, but she stops when the show says they think this presidential election is going to be one of the closest races in decades. Her breath hitches when dude says local turnout in our area could be "especially impactful."

"See? Your vote is *vital*," she says, pulling the plates from under our noses as she fusses at us to finish getting ready for school.

Ma is a teacher, so she has school, too. But I guess she doesn't trust me to go vote after my last class, so I'm off to the polls before homeroom.

"Hey, Ma, I got a gig tonight, so I'm gonna grab food with the band." I keep talking when I see the look on her face. "But we go on at eight, so I'll be home to watch results come in. Cool?"

She doesn't think it's cool, but I'm eighteen now, so she can't really do anything about it. Ma's not the type for You Live Under My Roof talks. She's better at the What Would Julian Do guilt trips.

Man, I can't wait to get in that voting booth. If only so the guilt trip will stop.

MARVA

I CAN'T BELIEVE HOW LONG THIS LINE IS. I DON'T care how nerdy I look—I can't stop the giant smile that's spreading across my face as more and more people join behind me.

I'm at the very front, of course. Armed with my first coffee of the day and my completed sample ballot, though I know all the candidates and measures I'm choosing by heart. I'll be in and out in ten minutes. I have this so perfectly timed that I'll still get to school with twenty minutes to spare.

I check my phone, but still no text from Alec. What the

hell? I guess technically it's my turn to respond, but what he's doing is unacceptable. How can he just change like this when he's been my boyfriend for more than two years?

I glance behind me to see how the line is shaping up. It's mostly people my parents' age, but there are a few younger ones, too. No other high school kids, though. I'd like to think that's because they're all coming after school, but I'm not that naive. All that time I spent canvassing, phone-banking, and text-banking made it crystal clear just how many people want nothing to do with implementing change in this world.

The guy about a dozen people back might be my age. He's so tall, though, it's hard to tell. He has light brown skin, close-cropped reddish-brown hair, and big hands that keep drumming a rhythm on his thighs. He's wearing giant black headphones, and I wonder what he's listening to as I turn back around.

The front door to the church opens and a gray-haired woman with a sunny smile props it wide with a doorstop.

"Morning, folks, and happy Election Day! The polls are officially open."

I swear, I get the chills.

The women behind the check-in table greet me with a smile and point me to the voting booth. I stop and stare.

It's not the first time I've been in one—I've gone with Mom and Dad several times over the years. But this is all me. *My* decisions. *My* chance to try to change the things I'm sick and tired of, just like my hero, Fannie Lou Hamer.

"Everything okay?" asks the woman sporting an auburn braid that trails over her shoulder.

"Oh—yes, sorry." I sip from my coffee and smile. "I'm just so excited to be here. This is my first time voting."

She smiles back. "Good on you, doing your part."

Oh, lady. If you only knew.

I step into the booth and take a deep breath. To orient myself in this moment, but also to take in every part of the voting experience. It smells . . . musty. I insert my ballot like the woman instructed and flip open the guide. All the propositions and candidates are there, just like I memorized weeks ago. But I can't help going through each one to make sure the issues I'm really here for are still there. Things my parents say this country has been fighting over for decades: healthcare, gun control, climate change, social justice. . . . Things that should have been *solved* decades ago. I take my time to read each paragraph and carefully fill in the circles on my ballot, a surge of pride coursing through me with each vote I make. I don't know how Alec can say this doesn't matter.

When I'm done, a man with round glasses takes my ballot and feeds it into the machine. "Thank you for voting," he says, handing me a giant sticker that says I VOTED. I immediately peel it off, press it over my heart, and say, "Thank *you*."

I must have taken longer than I thought, because the guy with the headphones is standing at the check-in desk, talking to the red-braid woman. His headphones are looped around his neck now. The woman scans the list all the way from top to bottom, page to page, until she gets to the end. She looks up at him and shakes her head.

"Sorry," she says, her face sincerely full of apology. "You're not on the list."

DUKE.

"WHAT? ARE YOU SERIOUS?"

Shit. This can't be happening. Not after Ma's breakfast lecture, and the memories of Julian, and Ida's complaining all the way here. I just want to get through this day, get to my gig, and kick ass on my drum solo.

No way in hell am I going home without that damn I VOTED sticker. But more than Ma, I'm scared of Julian. I don't believe in ghosts, but I'm pretty sure he'll find some way to haunt the shit out of me if I don't get this done.

The woman with red hair puts her hands up and looks

at the line behind me. "I don't know what to tell you. You're not on the list. Is it possible you're—"

"What's going on here?"

With that tone, I figure some mom is stepping in to help, but when I turn around, it's a girl my age. I squint at her. It's the girl who was standing at the front of the line when I got here. I thought maybe she was a volunteer. Something about her looks official, like all she needs is a clipboard and nobody would ever question what she's doing.

"Excuse me?" says the woman at the table, eyebrows all bunched up.

"You said he's not on the list?" The girl looks at me now, her brown eyes flashing. "Are you registered?"

"Yeah . . ." I say slowly.

She turns back to the woman. "Then what's the problem?"

"I'm sorry, who are you?"

The girl lets out the biggest, most exaggerated sigh, and I can't help it. I laugh.

She glares at me. "This isn't funny!" Then, to the woman: "I was *just* here. First in line to vote, remember?"

The woman sighs and leans back in her seat. I adjust my headphones around my neck, looking back and forth between the two of them.

"I'm Marva Sheridan," the girl snaps. "I already voted. *My first time.* And maybe this would be his first time, too." She looks at me for confirmation. I nod. "This is *his* first time, too. You can't deny him this right."

I feel bad for laughing. She's so serious about this, like the girl version of Julian, minus the dreads. I look at her a little closer and realize she's kind of cute. Even with that hard look on her face. She's shorter than me. Then again, everyone is shorter than me—I've heard enough basketball comments to last about ten lifetimes. But she barely comes up to my shoulder. Her skin is this nice dark shade of brown, and she has black braids hanging down her back with one bright pink one looped over her right ear.

"Hey," I say softly, glancing at the woman behind the table before I look at her. Marva. "It's okay. You don't have to do this."

"It's actually not okay. . . ." She pauses, clearly wanting to use my name but not wanting to ask for it.

With anyone else, I'd probably make them sweat a little because I can kind of be a dick like that when I want to be. People take shit too seriously most of the time, and it's fun reminding them. But she just looks so damn earnest, and I don't know why, but I somehow feel like the wrong word could make this entire day crumble for this girl I've never met.

"Duke," I say. Then I add, "Crenshaw."

I know her first and last name. Only seems fair.

She blinks like she wasn't expecting that and tugs on the pink braid as she says, "It's actually not okay, Duke. Have you heard of voter suppression?"

The woman behind the table sighs again, clearly not appreciating the scene unfolding in front of her. We're backing up the line and it's not even seven thirty. She does another scan of the voter roll. "Are you sure you're registered in this jurisdiction?"

I think back to when I registered. Or *pre*registered, when I was sixteen. The same year we moved here . . . when we were using Dad's address for everything.

Shit.

"What?" Marva says, fingers thrumming against her hip. Damn. Can she see all this from my expression?

"I, uh . . . I might be registered somewhere else." My eyes sweep from her braids down to her black combat boots. "My dad's address."

The woman nods, already looking past us. "Would you mind stepping aside so I can check people in?"

Marva marches out of the church, a dark storm cloud

practically appearing above her head. Outside it's crisp but bright.

"Hey, thanks," I say, looking toward the parking lot where Ida's waiting in my car. "I'm just gonna go after school, but I, uh, appreciate you fighting for me like that." I feel like I need to say something else to give this a proper ending, so I mutter, "Have a good day."

Jesus. Like she's working a drive-through or ringing me up at the drugstore.

But before I can take a step, there's a tight grip on my arm. She may be small, but she's strong.

"Listen, we have to try to figure this out," she says, the desperation in her voice damn near palpable. "I didn't spend *months* helping people register and educating them on the ballot measures only to see someone throw away their vote."

I frown. "I'm not throwing it away. There's nothing to figure out. I told you, I'll go after school. Got plenty of time before my gig."

Her eyes narrow at the word *gig*, but it doesn't deter her. "How do you know you'll be registered there? You can't just wait hours to find out. The lines will be out of control. Don't you care about democracy?"

Has she been talking to my mom?

"I gotta go," I say, backing away. "Killer test in Calculus, third period. I'll figure this out. I promise. Peace."

I half expect her to tighten the grip on my arm, but she lets me go freely. No doubt glaring, but once I turn around, I don't dare look back to check.

Ida is waiting in the passenger seat, furiously texting. She glances over as I get in next to her.

"Who was that girl you were talking to?"

I toss my headphones in the backseat and look out the windshield. Marva is still standing there, now focused on her phone. At least she didn't follow me over here. Except... the more I look at her, the more I wonder if I should've just agreed to let her help me. I can't miss that calc test, but she *is* really cute. Cuter than any of the girls at my school. And she's maybe the most intense stranger I've ever met, but it's kind of dope that she cares so much about something when she doesn't even know how it's going to turn out.

I shake my head, looking at the clock. I gotta go if I'm going to get us to school on time. I put the key in the ignition and turn. The car stutters like it did this morning and yesterday and the day before that. I've been meaning to get it to the shop, but usually, it starts.

Not this time.

I turn that key over and over again, but the car just chokes and stutters until Ida looks at me and says, "I don't think the sixteenth time is the charm."

I try once more. Sending up a prayer to anyone who'll listen. And . . . nothing.

Shit.

MARVA

STILL NO TEXTS FROM ALEC.

I look at the last one he sent, as if it will magically turn into something else. Something like *Of course I'm voting, Marv. Just messing with you.* Or *Give me one more reason why I should support this two-party system and I promise I'll get to the polls.*

But I'm starting to wonder if it would even matter if he texted. He hasn't been himself lately. He's still the same Alec, sweet and attentive, but something is off. We used to spend all night discussing things like the policies that most resonated with us, and the best way to get the word out about our candidates. Now he changes the subject almost every time I bring up the election. My stomach twists into a knot when I think about the disagreement we had a couple of months ago. I couldn't believe I was talking to my boyfriend of nearly two and a half years. I still can't.

"Hey."

I jump and turn around, almost dropping my phone. It's the guy who's probably not going to vote either.

I didn't even hear anyone come up behind me, which is so not like me. Mom says I have superpowers when it comes to sound. I can hear the trash trucks when they're blocks away and we forgot to drag the bins out to the curb, and Selma when she's in a playful mood, slinking around the house so she can pounce on one of us when we walk around a corner. I can even hear my parents murmuring about me in the kitchen when I'm doing homework all the way down the hall in my room. Nothing bad, really. They just think I'm too serious for my age and that I should be "having fun" instead of focusing so much on college applications and raising awareness for the election. I want to tell them this *is* fun for me, but I don't want to face that look in their eyes—the one that says they're way cooler than their own daughter.

I stare at him, clutching my phone by my side. "Hi."

"Duke," he reminds me.

"I know," I say, rolling my eyes. It was only, like, five minutes ago that he walked away from me like I was trying to get him to join a cult instead of helping him find the proper polling place.

"So, uh, do you have a car here?"

I narrow my eyes. "Why?"

He sighs. "Mine won't start. Was thinking maybe you could give me a jump? I gotta get my little sister to school, and I—"

"I know, I know." I drop my voice to mimic his: "Killer test in Calculus."

He frowns. "You don't go to school or something?"

"Of course I go to school."

"Exactly. You seem like someone who'd take it pretty seriously, so I don't know why you're giving me shit about needing to be there."

I look down at the blank screen on my phone and shove it in my bag. I don't look at him as I take a sip of coffee. "I'm just... Today is really important, okay? And sometimes it seems like I'm the only person who actually cares about the future of our country."

He laughs, but it's not like the one from before. Not exactly. This one is gentler. Less mocking. "Are you kidding? You saw how many people were in line back there. Look at it now—wrapped around the building. And the parking lot is full."

My eyes skate over the church and all the cars baking in the sun. He's right. But I don't want to give in that easily.

"Well, sometimes I feel like I'm the only person *our age* who cares."

"I was in that line, too."

I chew on the inside of my lip for a moment. "I have a car, but I don't have jumper cables. Do you?"

"Nah." His big shoulders sag. "All right. Thanks anyway. I'll call a car or something. You think the church will tow me if I leave mine here for the day?"

I glance at my phone again, checking the time. I *do* take school seriously, but I don't have any tests or quizzes today. I could probably miss two weeks straight and still graduate at the top of my class. Which I'd never do, even if all the hard work I've put in over the years gives me some cushion. So it feels as if someone else has taken over my voice box when the next sentence comes out of my mouth.

"I'll drive you."

He raises an eyebrow. "You don't even know where I go."

"Flores Hills isn't *that* big." If he doesn't go to my

school, he must go to one of the other two private schools in the area. I'm surprised I haven't seen him around before, but I'm so busy with academics that I don't have time to go to games or anywhere else I'd interact with people from other schools. "Laguna Academy?"

"Nope. Good ol' Flores Hills High."

"Oh." He laughs again, and it makes my cheeks warm. "What?"

"The look on your face is like I said I went to school in the gutter."

"It is not." But I don't say it so much as huff it, and then I'm even more embarrassed.

"We're not all hooligans and hoodlums at FHH," he says, and I swear his grin gets bigger the hotter my face burns. "Just some of us."

Ugh. Who even says *hooligans*? "Do you want a ride or not?"

"Yeah, but Ida has to come, too."

"Who's Ida?"

"Me," says a cheerful voice over my shoulder.

I jump, completely startled again. I might need to get my hearing checked.

DUKE

MARVA DRIVES LIKE A MANIAC.

From the minute we merge onto the freeway, people start honking. She's not a bad driver, just the most aggressive one I've seen in a long time. You can only be so chill on the freeway, but she jerks the car around like literally everyone is in her way. I grab the oh-shit bar on the passenger side as she cuts off a silver BMW by inches.

"You know, it's cool if we're a few minutes late," Ida says from the backseat. She's finally detached her nose from her phone, so even she must be worried about the fate of our lives.

Marva glances at her in the rearview mirror. "What?"

"You seem like you're in a hurry, so... you know. We can get a late pass or whatever. You don't have to drive so fast."

Marva laughs. "You think this is fast?"

Ida stares at me with wide eyes when I look back at her between the seats.

"So, where do you go to school?" I ask Marva, hoping she might slow down if I distract her a bit. But not too much. Just enough to get us to FHH in one piece.

"Salinas Prep," she says, laying on the horn when someone cuts *her* off for once.

"Damn."

"What?"

"It's just... fancy."

She shrugs. "It's really not."

But everyone in this car knows she's lying. Salinas Prep has some ridiculous statistic, like 70 percent of their students go to the Ivy Leagues. I don't even have to ask to know that she's applying early acceptance, and probably every single school is out of state.

Nothing against Ivies, but I don't get the big deal. I just don't understand why anyone would pay all that money to go to a place where people think they're better than you because they were born into rich families. I like school, but I don't think I need to apply someplace where secret societies and legacy admissions count more than what you actually bring to the table as a person.

"A girl in my class is going out with someone from Salinas Prep," Ida pipes up. "Do you know Aileen Mayer?"

"The name sounds familiar," Marva says. I can't tell if she's pretending not to know her or if she really has no idea who she is.

"I met her at a protest I went to recently," Ida says.

I can feel my sister's eyes on me without even turning around. But she swore me to secrecy, so I know not to say a word about that protest. Even in front of Marva, who'd probably respect her for what she did.

"She's pretty badass. And involved in, like, a million things. Orchestra, cheerleading, an officer in the GSA." When Marva doesn't respond, Ida adds, "The gay-straight alliance?"

Marva sighs. "I know what the GSA is. Her name doesn't sound familiar, but my boyfriend's best friend runs the meetings. Maybe he knows her."

My jaw tenses. Hard. It comes out of nowhere, and

I'm glad Ida is in the backseat and not sitting next to me. My little sister notices everything. Even when she's on her phone.

"Who's your boyfriend's best friend? And your boyfriend? I bet Aileen knows them, too."

"He's nobody," Marva snaps, pushing down hard on the brakes behind a slow-moving pickup truck.

Out of the corner of my eye, I see Ida shrink down in her seat. And she gets on my nerves worse than just about anybody I know, but that doesn't mean I want total strangers being an ass to her.

"You seem pretty stressed," I say to Marva, trying not to let my voice get too annoyed. It gets deeper when I'm annoyed, and it's so deep it kind of booms, and it makes people nervous when a Black dude my size starts talking in a booming voice. "You can take the next exit and drop us off at a gas station or something. We'll call a car the rest of the way."

Marva takes a couple of deep breaths, staring straight ahead at the stalled traffic. Then she looks in the mirror at Ida. "It's been a day."

"It's not even eight o'clock," Ida shoots back.

"It feels like midnight," Marva mumbles. She pauses, then says, "I'm sorry, okay? His name is Alec Buckman.

And... it's cool that you go to protests. I tried, but I get too angry at the counterprotesters, so my parents figured it was best if I used my voice in other ways."

Ida shrugs, traffic starts again, and the car is silent as Marva shuttles us to school. It might be my imagination, but I think she drives a little slower, too.

She swings the car into the circle drive at 8:05, five minutes before the late bell. Ida grabs her bag, calls out a hurried thanks to our chauffeur, and slams the door, running up to the building without waiting for me.

"Good luck," Marva says, her eyes fixed on the dashboard.

"With my test?"

"Oh, yeah. That too."

But I know she was talking about getting to my polling place. I'm pretty sure voting is the only thing that's been on her mind all week... maybe months.

I grip my bag and look at the school. The first time Ma dropped me off here, FHH looked like a monster. It's so much bigger than my old school, and Ma kept calling it a campus, which made me think of college, and I broke out in a cold sweat. I'd shot up four inches over the summer to six three, and I didn't know what I was more afraid of—people knowing I was just a scared punk of a sophomore or them thinking I was a senior who knew a lot more than I did. I guess I shouldn't have been so nervous, knowing Kendall went here . . . but that was stressing me out, too.

I glance at Marva again. "Thanks."

"Uh-huh." She puts her hand on the gearshift like she's going to throw this thing into drive and gun it as soon as I get out. From what I've seen, she probably will.

But for some reason, I can't make myself open the door. "Where you off to now?"

She gives me massive side-eye. "My *fancy* school. Where else?"

"You have a test?"

"What's up with all the questions?"

I clear my throat. "I, uh, was wondering if the offer still stands?"

She finally looks at me, her eyes narrowed but curious. "What offer?"

"To help me find my polling place." What the hell am I doing? I've already seen how she drives. Yeah, she's kind of cute, but what if she's a serial killer? I have a test today. And she's got a boyfriend. I wouldn't want my girl running around with some strange dude . . . if I had a girl.

But for the first time all morning, there's something

almost like a smile on her face. “Really?” Then she goes serious again, quick. “What about Calculus?”

I raise my shoulders and drop them. “I’ll figure it out.”

I’m eighteen, so I don’t need my parents to sign off on my absences. I’ll pretend I got food poisoning from breakfast (sorry, Ma) and beg Ms. McDonagh to let me retake it. She likes me, so I shouldn’t have to beg too hard. I hope.

“Oh.” Marva sits up straight, pulls on that pink braid, and gives me a real smile. “Okay, then. Let’s roll.”

I shake my head, laughing at how unnatural that sounds out of her mouth. “Yeah. Let’s roll.”

MARVA

I SHOULD FEEL WEIRDER ABOUT SITTING WITH A strange guy at Drip Drop Coffeehouse on a Tuesday morning.

I try not to think about what Alec would say if he saw us. He's been acting strange about the election lately, but he's still very much my boyfriend. I wouldn't want him thinking that I was doing anything to sabotage us. What we have is too good.

"What do you want?" Duke asks, staring at the giant chalkboard menu as he stands.

"Oh, I can get my own." I unzip my bag to find my wallet.

"I got it. Least I can do since you're helping me."

"No, really—"

He gives me a long look. "Marva? I got it. What do you want?"

"An Americano with two shots," I mumble.

"That what you had this morning?"

I nod. It feels like I stopped at Drip Drop a million years ago instead of two hours.

"Damn," he says, shaking his head as he goes over to wait in line.

I sigh as I pull out my phone. He's not the first person to judge my coffee consumption, and he won't be the last. But I don't drink, or smoke cigarettes or weed. I have to have *something.*

I look at Duke standing at the counter. He seems to be getting taller each time I look at him. What is it like to be that tall? I wonder if he plays basketball.

While he's waiting, I pull up the new photos of Selma. I try to snap all her pictures in natural light, but it was too dark this morning, so she's lit by the lamp of my bedroom. I had to take them first thing to commemorate

Election Day. I'll shoot more later with her wearing my voting sticker.

Keeping one eye on Duke as he approaches the counter and starts to order, I log into Selma's social media and upload the most adorable photo. She's sitting in the floofy folds of my duvet before I made the bed, looking absolutely angelic. I set a filter to make it sharper and brighter, caption it *Happy Election Day!*, and post it just as Duke puts his wallet back in his pocket and steps off to the side to wait for our drinks.

By the time he comes back to the table a few minutes later, the photo already has 336 likes. I used to worry about getting too political on her account. Selma is the only one I ever feature in the photos; people are 100 percent there for cute cat content. But one day, on a high from phone-banking, I came home with a campaign poster, posed her in front of it, and uploaded the photo before I could think too much about what I was doing. People loved it. Their comments were similar to what they're posting today:

Happy Election Day, Eartha Kitty!

Cutest election kitty ever

Eartha Kitty, are you voting today?

I quickly close out of the app as Duke slides my cup toward me. "One Americano, two shots."

"Thank you." I do a double take at the mountain of whipped cream topping his mug. "What is that?"

He settles his long body into the chair across from me, knees jutting off to the side. "Hot chocolate."

"Really?"

"You look like you've never seen anyone order a hot chocolate."

"Well, I haven't. Not anyone over the age of ten, anyway."

Duke makes a face. "Should I get five shots of espresso so you'll respect me?"

"You can start with three." I smile so he'll know I'm kidding. His face relaxes.

"So, how are we going to figure out where I'm voting?" he says, slurping at the whipped cream.

"Well, what's your dad's address?" I pull up the site for a polling place locator on my phone and push it toward him so he can type it in.

He stares at the phone for so long, the screen goes dark. I wave a hand in front of his face. "Hello?"

"Sorry, I... I don't think I know my dad's address."

I blow on my coffee. "Did he just move?"

"No . . . I'm just not there a lot." He clears his throat and digs his own phone out of his pocket. "Hang on, I can find it."

I look around Drip Drop as he starts typing and swiping. I've lived here my entire life, but it still astounds me how many people who aren't at work during the day are consistently decked out in designer clothes, climbing out of Teslas and Porsches. It's a Tuesday morning and the place is packed. I check every single person to see if they're wearing voting stickers. Only about half of them pass my test.

"Okay, got it," Duke says, and types the address into the site on my phone. His face drops immediately.

"What?" I ask before I take a sip of coffee, hoping it's finally cooled enough.

"It's at Flores Hills Elementary . . . where my mom works."

DUKE

"SO?"

I look up at her. "*So?* I should be in homeroom right now."

"Yeah, but you're skipping for a good cause. And the elementary school isn't too far. We *could* even have you back in time for Calculus if traffic agrees with us."

I squint at her. Does traffic *ever* agree with her? But I can't help feeling relieved that it's this easy. I showed up to the wrong spot, we found the right one, and I might even make it back in time for my test. Even though that last part doesn't exactly make me feel better.

"Why do you look like that?" she asks, tapping a finger against her coffee cup. Her nails are short. I wonder if she bites them like I do.

"Like what?"

"Confused."

I shrug. "I think this might just be my face."

Marva laughs, picking up her phone. She stares at the screen for a moment, then looks at me. "Should we check to make sure you're registered? Just in case?"

"Nah. I preregistered a couple of years ago. I just showed up to the wrong spot, and now we got the right one."

She nods and drinks more coffee. I don't miss the skeptical look in her eyes, but I feel like that may just be her normal face, too.

"So, if you've been preregistered since you were sixteen, that must mean your family is pretty political."

"Understatement of the year," I mumble, swiping a finger through the hill of whipped cream in my cup and licking it off in one quick movement.

Marva cocks her head to the side. "Really? Are they, like, *actual* politicians?"

"Nah, but my brother probably would've been. If he . . ."

"What? What happened?"

"He died." I say it like it's a fact, because it is. But it's still weird as hell to me that it's something I say now. That it's something I've been saying for two years, something I'll be saying for the rest of my life: *My brother died.*

"Oh." Marva looks down at her Americano, hands wrapped around the cup like it's a cold winter day instead of the sunny, seventy-five-degree fall day that's normal in our town. "I'm so sorry."

"It's all right. It was two years ago."

A slight frown pinches her face. "Two years? That's, like, no time."

"Yeah... well."

"Were you close to him?"

We're in the middle of a busy-ass coffee shop with moms and dads and strollers and people typing away on laptops, but it's suddenly too fucking quiet in here. I wish I'd brought my drumsticks. At least then I'd have something to distract me.

"Yup," I say quickly. "I was."

There are very clear Before and After moments when someone hears about Julian. Before, they feel fine thinking whatever they think about me. Even if they don't know anything at all. But after... that's when all the backtracking starts. You can practically see it on their faces, the worry that they've done or said something that might be offensive to the guy who has a dead brother.

"I've never known anyone who died," she says slowly. "I mean, nobody who was young and that I was close to. . . ."

"It's a trip. Do not recommend." I clear my throat and change the subject so I won't have to see her slide too far into the After. "What about your family? They all take this stuff as seriously as you do?"

"*This stuff?*" Marva shakes her head. "Duke, *this stuff* is going to affect our lives for years. And our kids' lives, too."

My eyes almost pop out of my head. "Kids? Damn, you already thinking that far ahead?"

"It's impossible not to! Glaciers are melting, sea levels are rising way too fast, and droughts, catastrophic hurricanes, and epic floods are becoming *normal*. Not to mention the growing amount of unchecked bigotry and hate crimes and school shootings . . . I mean, honestly, I don't even know if I *want* to bring kids into this world with the way things are going."

I take a long drink of hot chocolate. It goes down thick and sweet, and I lick the whipped cream off my mouth before I speak again. "How long you been thinking about this stuff?"

"Forever, I guess? But the last election, when we were fourteen...that was sort of my breaking point. Like, I *knew* I had to start working to make sure things change, or I'd never be able to forgive myself. I can't just sit back and watch this world go to shit, you know?"

Her words send a shiver through me. This is the same kind of stuff Julian used to say. Almost verbatim. It's not like I'm dumb enough to think my older brother was the only person who cared about voting this much. I knew his friends, who were all involved in some type of activism. They used to sit around our kitchen table for hours, talking about these things while Ma listened—sometimes contributing and most of the time making way too much food for their unofficial meetings.

"Have you ever thought about being a community organizer?"

"Not really?" she says. "I mean, I'm planning to go to school, and I'm probably going to be there for a while."

"I know you're not trying to be a professional student."

"No, but I'll probably go to law school."

"You really do have your whole life planned out, huh?"

She slurps down the rest of her coffee and pushes the cup away, standing up. "If I don't plan it, who will?"

MARVA

MY PHONE PINGS WITH A TEXT AS SOON AS I unlock the doors to my car.

"This is a rich-person car," Duke observes as he opens the door to the passenger side.

I look down at my phone. It's Alec. Finally.

"Truth hurts, huh?" Duke continues.

I look at him over the top of my car. "What?"

"That you go to a fancy school and drive a rich-person car," he says, smiling before he ducks into the seat.

"What are you talking about?" I slide in next to him,

my fingers hovering over the phone screen. Since when am I afraid to look at texts from my boyfriend?

"Volvos. They're luxury vehicles by design."

"You don't even know me." I roll my eyes. "Why are you so obsessed with what I drive and where I go to school?"

His knees knock against the glove box as he settles himself in the seat. "You seemed embarrassed by it earlier. You don't need to be. It's okay if your parents have money."

"Who ever said it wasn't okay? And the car is old." It used to be my dad's, made in the nineties. It was vintage when he got it, and he drove it until I turned sixteen. When he couldn't bear to get rid of it, I told him I'd still drive it if I didn't have to deal with the maintenance. He was so thrilled, he couldn't say no to that.

"It's vintage," Duke says, as if he's reading my mind. "Look at this console—it has a tape deck!"

Something my dad is entirely too proud of, considering no one listens to cassette tapes anymore. I didn't even know what they were until he showed me his old collection. Another thing he can't part with.

"My family isn't rich. They just prioritize education."

"While mine decided to send me to Hooligan High, huh?" he asks, reaching for his seat belt.

I let out an exasperated sigh. "Are you going to keep doing this all day?"

"Maybe. It's fun. You get so flustered."

"I'm *not* flustered. And what if it was the other way around?"

He stops fiddling with his seat belt for a moment. "Huh?"

"I mean, what if I were the one teasing you about going to public school?"

"But why would you do that?" He looks at me like I've sprouted another head. "It's clearly a dick move. People with money have the upper hand."

"My parents are Black," I say in a voice that comes out a little too snippy. "They don't have the upper hand on a whole lot of things. Did you not get into Salinas Prep or something?"

"Ouch."

I know he's looking at me, but I'm a bit embarrassed by what I just said—and how I said it—and I don't look back.

"Did you ever think maybe some people *like* going to public school?" Duke says.

I don't respond. He continues.

"My sister and I went to private school in our old town. Julian gave my parents shit about it all the time, but they were afraid to send us to public school. Even though he got out of there alive, I think they thought we were too soft to handle it. Before we moved here, we looked at all the schools in the area, but I told them I wanted to go to Flores Hills High and Ida said the same about the middle school."

"Oh," I say in a quiet voice. I trace the edge of the steering wheel. We need to go, but I still haven't started the car. "It was that easy? Convincing them?"

"Julian had just died and we'd moved to a new town and their marriage was basically in the shitter. It wasn't too hard."

He's the one who brought it up—and kept bringing it up—so I'm not sure why I feel like such a huge jerk right now. I wonder if I should apologize, but when I look over at Duke, he doesn't seem mad. His face seems the same as always: vaguely content, and amused by something I can't figure out.

I look back down at my phone in my lap, trying to quell the embarrassment spreading through my body in waves.

Finally, I swipe Alec's text open to see if there's more than the preview showed.

There's not. It's just three words that manage to infuriate me way more than they should:

Where are you?

ABOUT ALEC.

I HEARD ABOUT ALEC BUCKMAN AT MY SALINAS Prep orientation a full week before I actually saw him.

He'd attended the lower school, so everyone knew him. Even the new kids who were starting freshman year, like me. I heard about how he was *so cute* and *so charming* and *so smart*, and this was according to just about every other girl and several guys I met.

I won't lie—they weren't wrong, from what I could tell. He was in honors courses, and I guess he was kind of cute. A white guy with a mess of brown curls, gray eyes, and a wide smile. We had three classes together, but I didn't talk to him, so I couldn't confirm the charming part. I was almost certain that dimple in his right cheek had something to do with it.

Freshman year was...not my best. I usually do well at whatever I set my mind to, and that was true with academics. My grades were impeccable. But I couldn't seem to crack the code for fitting in at Salinas Prep.

I wasn't on scholarship, but I'm sure everyone thought I was. The lack of brown skin at my new school was more than noticeable, and even though I kept my head down those first few days, trying not to draw too much attention, I'd seen a few of the sympathetic looks cast in my direction. And I hated that. My parents do all right between Mom's job at the hospital and my father's position as a marketing executive, but I was well aware that most of the kids I went to school with were in a different tax bracket than my family.

I was friendly with a few people in my classes, and I ate lunch with the same small group every day, but nobody ever asked me to hang out after school or on the weekends. Everyone seemed to have their groups. Salinas Prep starts at kindergarten, so some kids had been going there their whole lives, moving up through the lower school like Alec until they reached the upper school freshman year. Even the other freshmen who were new to the school seemed to fit in almost immediately, as if they'd been prepping for years.

I still had my friends from my old school, but things were a little weird with them, too. My two best friends, Ryan and Georgia, kept making jokes about how bougie I was for going to the fancy school, but soon the jokes stopped and then the texts tapered off and then we were barely seeing one another. Even after we'd promised on the last day of middle school that nothing would change.

It hurt seeing them online hanging out when I wasn't invited, so I finally muted their accounts and started following people and things that made me feel good: politicians fighting for legislation that meant something to me, Black academics who always managed to teach me something new, and accounts featuring nothing but adorable animals.

I hadn't thought much about Alec until I noticed these long, thoughtful comments on several posts from politicians I followed. I looked at the profile and was shocked to see ABuck1 was actually *the* Alec Buckman from Salinas Prep. He didn't have many posts on his own page; a few photos from middle school and one or two since I'd started there. But he was a prolific commenter, and he seemed tuned in to the rights of others who didn't look or live like him: Black people, girls and women, poor people.

I ran into him in the hallway the week before our midterms. I'd been studying in the library during lunch and was headed to drop off books at my locker before my next class. I don't know where he was coming from or where he was going, but I don't think I'd ever seen anyone walk down a hallway like that who wasn't a teacher. So comfortable, so sure that they belonged.

I think I was staring at him, because he looked at me curiously, then slowed down until he was standing in front of me with a grin. I should have looked away, or at least turned around to busy myself with my books. But for the first time ever, I was truly face-to-face with ABuck1, the brain behind all those smart posts online. So I just stood there. Staring like I'd never seen a guy before.

"Hey, Marva," he said in a warm voice. In fact, *everything* about him seemed warm. His eyes, his smile—I guess this was the charming part people talked about. I just hadn't experienced him turning it solely on me.

"Hey," I said.

"I'm Alec. Buckman," he added, and all I could think about was how ridiculous the moment was. Like there was any way on earth I didn't know his name.

"Um, yeah," I say. "We have some classes together."

"I know. But we've never talked." He cocked his head to the side, his smile never wavering. "Why is that?"

Then I did turn to my locker to slide my books onto the shelf. "I don't really talk to a lot of people here."

"Salinas Prep is pretty insular." He paused, like he wasn't sure he should say what he was going to say next. "Kudos, because I don't think I could handle starting here my freshman year."

I zipped my bag, closed my locker, and looked at him. "I'm surviving."

"Yeah," he said, his smile growing so wide it made my skin flush. "You are. Mind if I walk with you to English Lit?"

And just like that, after a chance meeting in the freshman hallway during lunch, Alec Buckman became my first real friend at Salinas Prep.

DUKE

"WHAT'S WRONG?" HER FACE IS SO DAMN EXPRESSIVE, it's hard not to notice.

She shifts in the driver's seat and sets her phone face-down on her lap. "Nothing."

Now I feel bad. "Sorry about the car stuff. I was just being stupid."

She looks at me, confused. "What?"

"I mean, looks like you just got some bad news, and I shouldn't have been giving you so much shit." I lightly drum against my thighs with my fingers.

"No, it's not that. It's just—" She breaks off, shaking her head. "It's really nothing."

"Okay. Doesn't look like nothing, though."

Marva sighs and leans her head back against the seat. "I can't complain to a guy about another guy. You never understand where we're coming from."

I raise an eyebrow. "Who's the *we* in this situation?"

"Girls. Women."

"Try me."

"It's my boyfriend. Alec." She spins the phone around on her knee. "He's being a real jerk right now. Acting like . . . He's acting like someone I don't even know."

Am I supposed to give advice about some dude I haven't met? I've never even had a girlfriend. "What happened?" That seems like a safe response.

"Do you really want to hear this?"

"If you want to tell me."

Marva tips her head toward the ceiling and closes her eyes. "Alec isn't voting. Like, he's registered and filled out his sample ballot, and he's still not voting. After months of campaigning with me and discussing how important this election is. And it's not like he only cared about it after we were dating. He was really into politics before we even got together.... That's a big reason I started liking him."

"What's his deal now?"

"He's suddenly concerned about voting in a two-party system."

I snort. "White guy?"

Marva's eyes fly open. "How did you know?"

"Because Black and brown people don't have that kind of luxury."

"Plenty of Black and brown people don't vote either," she says, her voice tight.

"Of course. But the reasons are different," I say slowly as my finger-drumming tapers off. "You're not the only one who knows about voting. Black and brown people vote more than we get credit for, first of all. We've stopped a lot of assholes from getting into office and voted out plenty, too."

She nods, as if to say, *Fair point.*

"But the people who don't vote... a lot of them think it's because their vote won't count. Or because they know the entire government is rigged against them. You can't blame them, can you?"

Julian and his friends used to talk about this a lot. They'd have huge, sweeping arguments just about every time they got together, whether at our house or one of theirs. Sometimes it got so loud and heated that I wondered if it was gonna come to blows, but they'd always walk outside or into another room to cool off before it got to that point. They always remembered they were fighting for the same thing.

"No, of course not," Marva says, sighing. "I just don't want you to judge him because he's white."

"Who said I'm judging? I made an observation." I shrug, looking out the windshield at a woman in yoga pants talking on a Bluetooth as she paces in front of Drip Drop. "And if it makes a difference, my mom is white."

It's funny to see who's surprised by that info, and then how they handle it. White people usually seem shocked, because I look like any other Black person they know—darker skin than theirs, curly hair. But Black people have different reactions. A lot will say they knew right away, others seem like they couldn't care less, and then there's the few who give me a look of betrayal, like my blood is tainted. They're usually the same people who say we haven't had a *real* Black president, just because our first one had a white mom.

Marva grabs her keys from the console, sliding her phone in their place. "How is that?"

"Having a white mom?" I grin. Leave it to her to have the most surprising reaction of all.

"Yeah. And a Black dad, right?"

"Right. Uh, I don't know. Fine, I guess? She's the only mom I know."

"Is it weird that they're divorced now?"

"Nah. I mean, not really. You'd have to be living on another planet not to see that one coming." I clear my throat. "But they didn't split up because of the interracial thing, if that's what you're thinking."

"That's not what I was thinking."

But she says it so quickly that it must be exactly what she was thinking.

The thing about my mom is that she knew what people thought about her when she got with my dad. She's been honest with us from jump, saying how it wasn't easy, even with people she thought were progressive and open-minded. But she also vowed not to be a white person who raised her mixed kids without knowing anything about Black culture, like our history and how to do our hair. She's not perfect, but she tries pretty fucking hard to do right by us.

"Things gonna be okay with you and your dude?"

"I don't know," Marva says quietly. "I'm almost

positive he thinks this is some small disagreement. That we'll be totally fine after the election. But . . . I'm not sure how I can look at him when I know he didn't even try to do his part."

"Maybe he'll come around if you just talk to him again," I say. "Sounds like you, uh, have a pretty good thing."

I don't know who I think I am, trying to give dating advice when I basically have the least experience ever with dating. Or talking to girls. Or fixing things when I mess up.

"Maybe," Marva says. But she doesn't look convinced.

Just as she's putting her keys in the ignition, she glances out the driver's side window and yelps. The Bluetooth woman is standing by the car, waving frantically at Marva.

"Mrs. Thomas?" Marva says, dropping her keys. They land with a metallic *thud* at her feet.

She closes her eyes and grumbles under her breath.

MARVA

MY DAD'S COWORKER, MRS. THOMAS, TAPS ON the glass, a grin splitting her face and a Bluetooth piece strapped behind her ear. I slowly push the ancient button to roll down the window and force myself to meet her smile with one of my own.

"Marva? I thought that was you!" She practically pokes her head into the car. "What are you doing here?"

Rhetorical questions should be banned.

"Um, just getting some coffee." I gesture toward the front of Drip Drop, as if that's the answer Mrs. Thomas is actually looking for.

"Oh, well, me too, though I really shouldn't." She gestures to her yoga pants. "I just got done with a workout, and this is totally counterproductive, but I will *always* choose coffee over one of those twenty-dollar juices."

I don't dare glance at Duke. The last thing I need to do is draw any more attention to him than necessary.

As if Mrs. Thomas is reading my very thoughts, she cranes her neck to see past me. "Hi, there!"

"Hey," Duke says, nodding at her. When I finally look over, I almost laugh at the bemusement plastered on his face.

"How do you two know each other?"

I stifle a sigh. I've known Mrs. Thomas almost half my life. A ten-minute conversation with her at the marketing firm's summer picnic is enough to leave me exhausted for days. She's not going to leave until I give her what she's looking for.

"Duke, this is Mrs. Thomas. She works with my dad. Mrs. Thomas, this is my friend Duke. We're on a mission for democracy."

Her perfectly plucked eyebrows knit together. "Excuse me?"

"Voting. He had some problems with his ballot, and I'm helping him."

"Oh, isn't that nice of you, hon!" She breaks into a smile again and pushes her chest out as she points to the I VOTED sticker on her tank top, her cleavage uncomfortably close. "I went early, *before* yoga. I was worried there'd be a line, but I got right in, filled in my circles, and was the first one to show up for class."

I have to stop myself from rolling my eyes. It doesn't seem fair that Mrs. Thomas has already cast a vote and been to yoga class and we're still trying to get Duke to the right polling place.

"Well, I'd better get going. That spa appointment won't wait forever." She gives me a conspiratorial wink. "I figured why not treat myself to a day off since I've done my part today, you know?"

"But there's more you could do," I blurt before I know what I'm saying.

I bite my lip. When we first started getting to know each other, Alec thought it was so cute how I do that sometimes. *You're so passionate*, he'd say, giving me a soft smile. And it felt special. Like he'd never smiled at anyone but me that way.

"What was that, hon?" Mrs. Thomas says.

"It's just that, well, if you have the day off, you could

always see if anyone in your neighborhood or at senior centers needs a ride to the polls. Or—"

"Oh, I'm so sorry, hon," she says, tapping her Bluetooth. "I've got a call coming in and need to take it."

"But, Mrs. Thomas—"

She's snaking her head out of my car, though, just as fast as she slid into our space. "Tell your parents I said hello, though I'm sure I'll see your father at work tomorrow. Nice to meet you, DeAndre!"

Duke stares at her, openmouthed, as she power-walks to her giant SUV at the back of the lot. "Is she for *real*?"

I let out the sigh I was holding in the whole time she was standing here, but I don't feel any better. "Entirely. And she is absolutely going to tell my dad she saw me sitting in the car at Drip Drop with a guy when I should have been in school."

"Your folks gonna lose their shit?"

I shrug, trying to appear calmer than I feel. "I don't know. I've never skipped before."

Duke's jaw drops. "Wait, what?"

"Yeah. I... like school."

"Me too, but this isn't my first time skipping out on it."

He pauses. "Seems like we should do something special to commemorate it."

I look at him. "You want to celebrate my truancy?"

He shoots me a lazy grin. "Well, the first time only happens once, right?"

"You're ridiculous." I shake my head and finally turn the key in the ignition, checking my mirrors. "And we still have to get to the school and sort out this whole voting thing, remember?"

"Got it, boss," he says in the most serious of voices.

But when I look back over, there's a smile in his eyes.

"Thanks, *DeAndre*." I try to hide mine as I put the car into reverse.

DUKE

DUDE, HALF MY HOMEROOM IS COMING TONIGHT—we gotta kill

I stare down at Anthony's text, shaking my head like I'm coming out of a fog. Like this whole thing with Marva is happening in some existence outside my regular life. I usually can't think about anything except our gig the day of the show. Did I really just forget about it?

And then my mind goes where I've been trying to avoid going all day. I wonder if Kendall's gonna be there. She's the band's manager, so technically she's supposed to be at all our gigs. But with the way I handled things between us, I wouldn't be surprised if she quit just so she wouldn't have to see me outside of school.

Bet, I send back to Anthony, then reach into my bag to make sure my drumsticks are still there. It's corny, carrying them around like some asshole who wants everyone to know they're in a band. I don't take them out at school except for lunch, and only sometimes. Drumming calms me down. Gives me something to do with my hands and mind.

"What's that?" Marva asks without turning her head. She doesn't miss a damn thing, even when she's driving.

"Uh, just my sticks."

"Your what?"

"Drumsticks. I'm in a band."

A strange look comes across her face, like she's just stumbled on a complex math problem that's gonna take some time to process.

"What kind of band?"

"Indie rock? My boy Anthony raps on a couple of our songs, too, but we're mostly rock. For now. We're still trying to figure out our sound."

Jesus. Guess I need to get better at pitching us.

"Interesting," she says, looking both ways before

pulling the Volvo out onto the busy street in front of Drip Drop. "What's the name?"

"Promise not to laugh."

"I promise," she says with a straight face, her gaze focused on the car ahead of us.

"Drugstore Sorrow," I mutter.

Marva cackles so long and loud it makes me smile, too.

"So, you're shit at keeping promises. Good to know."

"I'm sorry," she says, finally catching her breath as she grips the steering wheel like it's the only thing holding her up. "It's just so *weird*. Where did you come up with that?"

"Our lead singer, Svetlana. She swears it's so memorable that we're going to have a huge following as soon as more people hear us play."

"I mean, no offense, but it sounds like she got it from one of those random band-name-generator sites."

I look away as Marva bites her lip. It's such a small gesture, probably something nobody but me would even notice. But it makes me think about her mouth and how I *like* her mouth . . . and then how she has a boyfriend, and I'm not supposed to be noticing and liking her lips like that.

"That's what I told her," I say, staring out my window instead. "She didn't exactly deny it."

"So, you play drums. That's pretty cool. Do you play in the school band, too?"

"Fuck that."

"Well, okay, then!"

"Sorry. I'm just not that into organized stuff like marching band or sports. I'd rather do my own thing. I'm self-taught, mostly. I've taken some private lessons, but I'm pretty sure I learn more by just banging it out on the kit at home."

"Who are your favorite drummers?" she asks, making a quick lane change to pass a slow-moving car.

My eyebrows go up. "You know drummers?"

"Not really. But you do."

"Dave Grohl, Neil Peart, Ringo, Elvin Jones," I rattle off. "But Questlove is probably my favorite."

"Why?"

"Well, he's dope as hell. Talented. Versatile. But he's also a big Black dude with a big 'fro, so I'm kinda biased." Even though I don't have a 'fro. Yet. Been thinking about growing it out, though.

She makes an abrupt stop at a red light. The kind of stop where Ma used to throw her arm across the passenger seat to make sure nobody was hurt, even if Ida and I were sitting behind her in our car seats. Marva doesn't seem worried about my safety, but she looks over. “Do you have any favorite *woman* drummers?”

“Sure. Sheila E. Cindy Blackman.” I pause. “Janet Weiss.”

Marva looks impressed for a whole two seconds before she frowns. “Well, you don’t deserve any awards for knowing their names.”

I laugh. “I know more than their names. Want me to go through their greatest hits? Best drum solos?”

“Maybe later. How long have you been playing?”

“A couple of years. My therapist suggested—”

I snap my mouth closed. Loose lips, man.

Marva doesn’t bat an eye, though. “Suggested what?”

I swallow. I usually don’t let that slip. Especially not with someone I just met.

“She, uh... suggested I take up something. A hobby. After my brother died.”

“Oh.” Marva’s eyes get big. “Right.”

The car feels way too quiet. I stare at the radio knob, wondering how pissed she’d be if I turned on something right now.

“I thought it was bullshit at first. Busywork so I wouldn’t realize how fucking shitty it was that my brother was gone. But music was the only thing that made sense, and drummers had always been my favorite. So I figured why the hell not." I twirl a drumstick in my left hand. "We have a gig tonight. Drugstore Sorrow. Our first paying one."

Marva raises her eyebrows. "A gig on election night? Bold."

"It's an all-ages show. I don't think most of the people coming to see us are gonna be thinking about voting."

It's pretty clear from the look on her face that she believes everyone should be thinking about it. And her voice . . . Every time she talks about voting . . . It's so full of . . . well, passion. Like she can't imagine anyone else not feeling the way she does about this. Like she'll work for the rest of her life to make sure they do.

"He'd like you," I say before I even realize the words are coming out of my mouth.

The light turns green, but she doesn't go right away. "Who?"

"My brother. Julian."

Marva still doesn't push on the gas, though. Not even when a car behind her honks.

"How do you know?"

I pause. "You're cut from the same cloth, my ma would

say. Julian was . . . determined. No matter how tough shit got. He never quit."

She swallows and looks me square in the eyes. "Thanks." Her voice is softer than I've heard it all day.

And, I think, a little proud.

ABOUT JULIAN.

SOMETIMES I COULDN'T STAND MY BROTHER.

It's not easy growing up in the shadow of someone who everybody thinks is damn near perfect. Julian didn't think that about himself. At least, *I* don't think so. He was always talking about how people and society are works in progress, and I'm pretty sure he counted himself in that, too.

But I've never seen anyone so selfless in my whole life. Sometimes it felt like he wasn't even real, let alone my brother.

He was seven years older than me. He used to call

himself the Great Experiment, because our parents waited so many years after he'd been born to have more kids. He thought it was because even though they acted all proud about their relationship and like they didn't care what other people thought, they were still freaked about bringing a mixed kid into this world. I think it's because he was so perfect they were worried other kids wouldn't live up to him.

Julian was cool to me, though. He never dismissed me just because I was so much younger.

I'll never forget this one time we went to McDonald's. He was watching me while Ma and Dad worked, and he told me we were going on a field trip. We met up with a couple of hard-looking dudes who seemed old at the time, but I later realized were probably about my age now. I was nine, and once Julian set me up with a Happy Meal and a game on his phone, I zoned out.

Later, in the car on the way home, I looked up from my game and turned to him. "Who were they?"

Julian stared straight ahead as he drove. "Amari and Tariq. I introduced you, remember?"

"Yeah, but who *were* they?"

He didn't say anything for a long time. I was starting to think he hadn't heard me when he finally answered. "Gang members."

My mouth dropped open. "They're in a *gang*?"

"Yup."

"Why were you talking to them?" I didn't know much about gangs, but I knew what they were and what they did, and that we weren't supposed to be talking to anyone who was part of them.

"Because I'm trying to build peace."

"They looked scary." I thought back to their skin covered in tattoos and the deep frowns embedded in their faces.

"People are complicated, little homie," Julian said, glancing over. "Nobody is all angel or devil. Dialogue between groups is good. Remember that."

I didn't get what he meant back then. I just thought he was brave. So brave that I bragged to Ma later about our field trip.

She lost her shit.

I was all tucked in my bed, lights out, when the yelling started.

"How *dare* you!" My mother's voice was louder than I'd ever heard it.

"Ma, calm down, okay? I—"

"*Calm down?* Julian, I am still your mother. And I'm *his* mother, too. How dare you sit him at a table with *gang members*. What were you thinking?"

"Ma." Julian's voice was as steady as our mother's was furious. "They're looking for some resolutions, too. They care about the community."

"If they cared about the community they wouldn't be doing all the things they do. It's shameful. And you're trying to reason with them?"

"You of all people taught me that everyone deserves a fair chance, Ma. Does that only count for certain people?"

"Julian."

"Change takes time. And patience. And . . . a willingness to listen to people we may not understand."

"What I understand is that you had your little brother eating a Happy Meal in front of some of the worst thugs in the county."

"Thugs, Ma? Really? Listen to yourself."

"You listen to me: Don't do this again. I know your intentions are good, but I will not have you endangering Duke's life."

It was quiet for a long time after that. Then came Julian's voice, defiant as ever: "What about *my* life, Ma?"

"You made it clear a long time ago that you're going to do what you want, Julian. It's up to you how you live your life."

MARVA

DUKE KEEPS SURPRISING ME. AND I DON'T LIKE IT.

I'm good at reading people. Figuring out their quirks and motivations—sometimes before they've even said a word. But every other fact out of his mouth gives me pause and he can see it and that makes me feel . . . out of control.

I should be thinking about how to respond to Alec instead of trying to figure out this guy I'll never see again after today.

Traffic is heavy on the way to the elementary school; Duke is preoccupied with his phone, and I'm glad. Maybe if I'm not distracted by him, my mind will clear and I can think calmly about Alec.

It's not like this is the first time we've ever disagreed about something. Alec and I are both strong-willed, and we're both used to getting our way with things. Me because I don't like to back down, and him because his parents weren't in the habit of telling him no when he was growing up. He *is* one of the rich kids from Salinas Prep that Duke was talking about, and he's not as bad as that stereotype, but he doesn't always rise above it.

Up until now, the biggest bump in our relationship was when we talked about colleges back in September. I assumed we'd be on the same page about where to apply, but I guess I also assumed I'd never be a girl who wanted to go to the same college as her boyfriend. Actually, I didn't really think I'd date at all in high school since I knew how much my parents were paying for me to go to Salinas Prep. I was planning to focus on my studies and get into a top school, *maybe* fitting in new friends if I found the time. Then Alec showed up in the middle of my very lonely freshman year, and all the plans I'd had for my high school career were rewritten.

We had a couple of casual conversations about college

over the summer. Then the discussions became serious as we realized how quickly time was moving.

"I don't want to apply anywhere you're not," he said, sitting across from me at my kitchen table one late August afternoon.

My eyes flew up to meet his. "Really?"

We'd been officially dating two years, since right before the start of sophomore year. We loved each other. I knew I didn't want to break up with him when we went away to school, but I hadn't been sure he felt the same way.

"Really." He twisted his fingers together and pulled them apart. "What do you think?"

"I think that's a great idea." I'd have to nix Howard and Mount Holyoke from my list. But if that meant I could stay with Alec—still see him every day, but with the freedom of a new state and dorms and no curfew—I believed it was worth it.

"Good," he said, reaching across the table to squeeze my hand. "That's really good, Marv."

We spent the rest of the afternoon going over the pros and cons of different schools, pulling up the websites to compare and contrast. Crossing off schools because they didn't offer programs we were both interested in. Or because one of us didn't like the weather. Or because

Jessa Bailey's brother went there and loved it and that automatically meant we should steer clear.

It was exhausting, but we got through it, and afterward, we were both satisfied with our comprehensive list. It felt good, looking at that list. Like we were on our way to becoming actual adults who could make compromises and hard decisions. We went out for burgers afterward to celebrate.

So I could have sworn I was sitting next to a different person a couple of weeks later when I looked over at his laptop and saw him plugging away at an application for a school we had explicitly decided *wasn't* on the list.

"What are you doing?"

Alec finished typing a sentence before he looked at me. "Filling out this app, babe. What's up?"

"But...that's not on our list."

He'd started typing again, but once he heard the tone of my voice, he stopped for good. Slid the laptop on the table and looked at me. "I know. Look, I wanted to talk to you about it—"

"When? After you got accepted?" I could hear my voice getting higher the more I talked, so I was sure Alec could, too.

"Marv...this is one of my dream schools. They have

one of the best political science programs in the country. I don't have to go if I get in." He hesitated. "But I can't *not* apply."

"So, what was the point of the list, then?"

He sighed, putting a hand over mine. "Marv—"

But I jerked it away. Scooted my chair back so that it scraped heavily against the floor. "You know those three weeks I spent there were absolute *hell*, Alec. It was only a couple of months ago. I still..."

Just seeing the name of that school again made my stomach hurt. I'd gone to a precollege program there over the summer, and it was truly one of the worst experiences of my life. Just like at Salinas Prep, I was one of the only Black kids on campus. But unlike our high school, the blatant bigotry was off the charts. It's incredible how many different ways there are to ask someone how they could have possibly gotten into *this* program. Or to ask if I lived in the projects. The first week, my roommate had asked point-blank if it's true that Black people don't wash their hair. I was ready to leave almost as soon as I'd set my bag down.

And Alec knew this. All of it. He'd listened as I vented to him over the phone, from thousands of miles away, and he'd consoled me as I broke down and cried to him on the really bad days. So it seemed like a done deal that he'd take it off his list when we'd finalized it a couple of weeks ago, before school started. The fact that he hadn't was gross and disappointing and... it made me feel like I didn't know him at all.

"Marv, I love you. I don't want *any* of this to end next year." His voice sounded tinny, like he was far away instead of sitting inches from me. "But I have to do this for me. Do you understand?"

"Don't patronize me. I *understand* that you're being selfish. You're not listening to me. That place is *toxic*. What if you do decide to go? I wouldn't be able to visit you. I wasn't being hyperbolic when I said I'd never set foot in that town again, let alone the campus."

Alec tried to touch me once more, this time on the shoulder. I flinched but didn't shake him off. "I am listening. You *know* I care about how you're treated. And I know things are different for you than they are for me... that you deal with shit I'll never have to experience in my life. But I have to do this. Just to see if they'd even take me. I'll never forgive myself if I don't."

I raised my chin. "Then I guess Howard and Mount Holyoke go back on my list."

"What? That's *two* schools I can't go to."

"You don't *have* to be Black to go to an HBCU."

Alec gave me a look.

"What? It's true. And anyway, I'm Black and a woman, so, yes. I get two schools catered to me to make up for that racist mess you can't let go of."

"Maybe we should talk about this another time," he said. "When we're not so . . ."

So what? Sure of what we wanted? Alec knew as well as I did that I'd never be okay with him applying there. And I knew he'd never have the nerve or desire to apply to an HBCU. The conversation was over, whether or not we wanted to admit it.

Next to me, Duke guffaws, bringing me back to the present. The backed-up traffic around us, the drumsticks resting on his lap, and his smell filling my car. Not a bad smell, but it's just . . . him. A soap or deodorant I don't know. Different from Alec.

"What are you looking at?" I ask, glad to take my mind away from my boyfriend.

"Do you know this internet cat?"

My whole body tenses. "Aren't there, like, a million internet cats?"

"I don't even like cats and I know this one. Her name is Eartha Kitty and she's . . . Well, I don't really know what she's famous for. But my sister is obsessed with her and keeps sending me posts." He shakes his head, holding out his phone. "I mean, how ridiculous is this? Who takes the time to do all these photo shoots with a cat?"

Thank god for stalled traffic because I'm pretty sure I'd crash my car otherwise, with him shoving a picture of Selma in my face.

"Totally ridiculous," I say, plastering on a smile. And trying not to look at the number of likes the picture has amassed since I posted. "Do you have any pets?"

"Nah, my dad was allergic, and Ma isn't really an animal person."

"What? I thought it was, like, mandatory for white people to like dogs."

I wait for his laugh, but when the silence stretches, I look over. He's frowning.

"What?"

"That's kinda low-hanging fruit."

"Joking about white people and dogs?"

"Yeah, it's like the same as joking about white people not seasoning their food. It's kinda tired, you know? And weren't you the one who didn't want me to judge your boyfriend because he's white?"

"Are you serious?" Now I'm frowning, too. "It was

a general joke. Not like I was actually picking on your mom."

"But you were, kinda."

And, by extension, that means I'm picking on him, too. Half of him.

I sigh. "Fine. Sorry. But please don't tell me Black people can be racist against white people. I'm not up for that right now."

"*O-kay*, but only if you promise not to school me on power structures and the difference between prejudice and racism."

I press my lips together, put my foot on the gas, and decide that doesn't even warrant a response. Even if that's exactly what I was about to do.

We drive the rest of the way to the elementary school in silence.

DUKE

ALL RIGHT, MAYBE I CAME AT HER A LITTLE WRONG.

Not gonna lie, I do get kinda hot when it feels like people are talking shit about Ma. It's like they think her being white wipes out the fact that she's still my mom.

But I don't really think that's what Marva was doing, even before I said what I said. Maybe I wanted to get her back for thinking I was judging her dude because he's white. And anyway, white, Black, whatever—what kind of dude doesn't get how dope she is? She's . . . a lot, but not in a bad way. She cares about things the way most people don't. Or are too embarrassed to show. Which is funny, because in the non-grossest way possible, she kinda reminds me of Ma.

We roll up in front of Flores Hills Elementary.

Ma.

My heart bangs against my rib cage like it's hitting a snare drum.

"Ready?" Marva says when she shuts off the car, her door already open.

"Not really."

Her eyes narrow. "Don't you dare try to tell me *you're* not voting now either."

I bust out laughing. "No, but I totally would've if I'd thought of it first."

"Oh my god," she huffs as she gets out and starts walking toward the school.

But I know I saw a flash of a smile in her eyes.

The first time I went back to my elementary after I'd moved on to middle school, I couldn't believe how tiny it looked. Like the halls were too small and the ceilings were too low, and even the doors didn't look wide enough for me to fit through. I didn't go to Flores Hills Elementary, but it looks small as hell.

As we pass by the office, I see a couple of kids sitting

on chairs across from the secretary's desk. They're so little their feet don't even touch the floor.

Marva walks fast to the parent center. I wonder if it's because she's ready for me to vote so she can get the hell away from me or if she can't wait to finish up with this so she can go drive people to the polls, like she was talking about. I tell myself it doesn't really matter if it's the first one. We're not friends—just associates, like Anthony would say. Never seen her before in my life, probably won't see her again after today.

But now that I know her . . . Well. I guess you could say I don't want to *un*-know her.

"Duke?"

My head snaps over at the sound of my name. Man, this school really *is* too small.

Ms. Amster pulls me into a hug before I can say anything. Except she's so much shorter than me that she's hugging my waist, so I just stand there kind of patting her back like a weirdo until she lets go. I see Marva watching from the corner of my eye, but I don't even think about looking at her.

"What are you doing here? Your mother will be so glad to see you!" Ms. Amster is the music teacher, and also my mom's best friend here in Flores Hills. She's cool, I guess, but she's the last person I want to see right now.

"Uh, actually, I'm not here to talk to her," I say, stuffing my hands in my pockets. "This is where I vote."

Her eyes move from my face to a point behind me, then to her hands and the floor. I want to ask her what she's looking at. Finally, she catches my eye again and says, "You're missing school for that?"

"It's a long story."

Marva clears her throat. It's small, but it digs right into my ear like a siren.

"But, uh." I scratch my arm. "Don't you think voting is a good reason to miss a couple of classes? It's kind of a big day."

Oh boy. Why'd I have to say a *couple* of classes? Ms. Amster eyes me in a way that I know means she's going to run right to Ma and tell her I'm here.

"Well, I'd better get going. Good to see you, Duke," she says before she heads toward the office. Her heels click a rhythm on the floor as she walks away. Sounds like the countdown to my inevitable lecture from Ma.

When I finally look over at Marva, she's smiling.

The parent center looks a lot like where I tried to vote in the church, except the walls are covered by bulletin boards pinned with event announcements and lists, inspirational posters, and a whiteboard with faded scribbles. There are only four voting booths, and they're cramped together, but there's a small table of people with lists in front of them, just like at the church.

Man, I hope that's the only thing that's like the church, though. If they turn us away here, Marva might have a breakdown.

"Who was that woman you were talking to?" Marva asks as we get in line.

There aren't a ton of people ahead of us, but there's more than I thought there'd be. I glance at the clock on the wall. They're in the middle of first period at FHH.

"Ms. Amster," I mumble in case anyone in here knows her. "My mom's friend."

"She's not voting," Marva says, bringing her hand up to examine her nails.

I stare at her, head cocked to the side. "What?"

"I can tell just by looking at someone. She's not voting."

"So you knew that lady at Drip Drop had already voted?" Because she damn sure didn't look like someone who would've been up in the voting booth first thing in the morning. Or ever.

"Mrs. Thomas? Yeah, of course. She's the type who votes because she doesn't want to *look* bad. She doesn't actually care about the issues, because most of them don't affect her and her family. But heaven forbid she get judged by someone in the school drop-off line, you know? So she does the bare minimum and slaps a sticker on her chest so people will know she did the right thing."

"Damn." I wonder if she's on her school's debate team. "But how do you know about Ms. Amster? She's always been pretty cool with me."

"Did you see the look on her face when you said why you were here? I've never seen anyone more shifty-eyed! Lots of people who don't give a shit about the state of their country are cool. But when push comes to shove—or, you know, just showing up and filling in some circles once every two years—lots of people don't actually show up."

I dunno. Ma is pretty militant about voting. I don't believe she'd be all right with her best friend not doing it.

"What if she was going to vote for the people you hate?"

Marva's lips curve into a surprised O. Has she never thought about this before?

I'm feeling pretty pleased with myself when she pulls her phone from her jacket. She frowns as she looks at the screen.

"It's my dad." She bites her lip for a minute, thinking,

and I take that chance to look at her without getting caught. She's pretty even when she's frowning. And I get the feeling she frowns a lot. She has today. But not just because she's upset—she frowns when she's thinking hard or judging what I said or figuring out what to say next. And I don't even know how this is possible, because I just met her, but I can tell the little difference in each one of them.

"Dad?" she says. "What's up?"

We inch ahead, one person closer to the check-in table.

"No, I'm not sitting down," she says. "What's wrong?"

I look over. That is for sure an upset frown.

MARVA

"DAD! WHAT'S GOING ON?"

He clears his throat a few times, and I can tell without even being there that he's pacing. I think I get most of my nervous energy from my father. Which is weird, because my mom has an incredibly stressful job. Not only trying to keep people alive and help them heal, but making them feel good and safe at the same time. It sounds exhausting, but I rarely see her sweat, even after a double shift. I bet Duke would make a good nurse.

"Marva, I'm so, so sorry. But . . . I just got back from my trip to New York and I left the front door open while

I was grabbing my luggage and the mail and . . . she's gone."

I frown. "What? Mom? Yeah, she had an early shift. She left before I did this morning."

"No, honey. Selma. She escaped."

My world tilts. With those two words, everything goes off-balance.

"Escaped?" I whisper.

"And I can't find her." My dad's voice cracks as he says, "I'm so, so sorry, honey."

"Dad, how . . . ? But she's never . . ."

"I don't know," he says quietly. "We've left the door open hundreds of times and she's never even attempted to leave. She always acted scared of the outside."

"Well, I can probably be home in"—I look at the line ahead of us; it's barely even moving—"thirty minutes?"

"No, honey, it's okay. I don't want you to leave school. She probably hasn't gone far at all. Probably just had the itch to see the world and she'll be right back."

I guess Mrs. Thomas hasn't called him if he thinks I'm still at school. But, honestly, I don't care if Mrs. Thomas told him she saw me having sex with a stranger in the parking lot of Drip Drop. All I care about is getting my Selma back.

"So you're going to just wait it out?"

"Marva, no. She's a member of the family. I'm going out to look for her now. I just don't want you to worry too much. I'll keep you posted, okay?"

I swallow hard, my throat thick from holding back tears. "Text or call me as *soon* as you know anything."

"I will, honey. I promise."

Duke is watching me as I hang up. "What happened?"

"My cat . . . she got out when my dad came home, and he can't find her." My voice chokes on that last word, but I take a quick breath and blink back the familiar sting in my eyes.

"Oh, man. I'm sorry. Do you need to go look for her?" He pauses, then: "Want me to come with you?"

"Oh." I don't know why I just assumed that if I were going to look for Selma, he'd come with me. It didn't even seem like a question in my mind. "No, it's okay. I mean, thanks. But my dad is going out to look for her now. I'm sure she hasn't gotten very far."

But I didn't really believe that when my father said it, and I'm not sure I believe it now.

ABOUT SELMA.

I NEVER WANTED A CAT.

It's not that I don't like them. I've always thought they're so regal, the way they move so haughtily and stand tall, wrapping their tails around their legs like at any moment someone could paint a portrait of them. And I've always admired their ability to intimidate people with a simple glare.

But with the exception of a couple of fish, we never had pets until Selma. My parents were very clear that they had no intention of getting me a dog or a cat only to have to take care of it themselves. And I liked my friends' dogs and cats, but I never felt a burning need to have my own. Or to clean a litter box.

Until Mom came home with that ridiculous black kitten my freshman year.

I was on my period, so I blame how fast I fell for Selma on my hormones being out of whack. But someone had found a litter abandoned in a cardboard box in the parking lot of the hospital, and she was so tiny, and when Mom walked in cradling her in a blanket, I immediately burst into tears.

"We're not cat people," I said as we watched her stumble across the blanket Mom had carefully placed on the living room floor.

"We're not *not* cat people," Mom said, perched on her knees at the edge of the blanket. "And she's not so small that we can't take care of her. The mother was nowhere to be found, but all the kittens' eyes were open, and they're able to walk."

As if on cue, the kitten got tangled up in her own feet and toppled to the side. I clapped my hand over my mouth, worried she'd hurt herself, but she hopped back up with a little *mew* and started toddling around again.

"Do you like her?" Mom asked, watching me.

"Of course," I said, though what I wanted to say was that I *loved* her. Instantly.

"Good. We know you've been having a tough time adjusting to your new school, and, well, an animal doesn't fix everything, but I figured it couldn't hurt to have a little companion around here."

I didn't say anything, but when I looked at her, she gave me a soft smile. And as embarrassing as it was to know my mom realized I was kind of a loser at my new school, it felt better than her not noticing.

When Dad got home, he joined us on the blanket, instantly smitten with her, too. We were too invested in our new family member to worry about dinner, so Dad ordered a pizza while Mom got a bowl of water and went next door to borrow cat food from the Cohens.

"She's so fluffy, I wonder if she's got some Maine Coon in her," my mother said, placing the bowl on the blanket. "We'll take her to the vet tomorrow."

The kitten lapped it up with her teeny pink tongue, ran around some more, and scrambled up to my lap, collapsing into a sudden nap. I stroked her soft dark fur as she snoozed, my heart melting into a puddle every time she let out a snore.

"Looks like she's chosen her favorite," Mom said, smiling at us cuddling. "You get to name her."

I knew immediately. "Selma," I said, gently scratching her back.

I had recently read about the 1965 march in Alabama to bring attention to voting rights for Black people. Selma was a beautiful name, but she deserved something iconic, too.

She mewed in her sleep and burrowed even farther into my lap. Approval, I think.

Mom nodded. "Selma. I like it." She bent down to rub her fingers over soft kitten ears. "Welcome to the family, Selma."

DUKE

TEN MINUTES LATER, WE'RE FINALLY AT THE head of the line.

I gotta admit, I was kinda nervous voting back at the church. Or *trying* to vote. I knew what I was supposed to do from going with Ma all those years, but realizing I was gonna be doing it myself for the first time was different. A pressure I'm not used to.

"Good morning," says the man behind the table. "Name, please?"

"Duke Crenshaw," I say, shaking away the déjà vu from earlier.

I'm holding my breath as his finger moves down the list in front of him, and when I glance at Marva, I think she is, too. The man frowns, shakes his head, and starts looking from the top once more.

Man, come on. This *can't* be happening again.

Marva's hands go up to her hips, ready for round two if it comes to that. But it won't. It can't. There's no way I won't be on this list. I triple-checked the location with Dad's address, and this is where we're supposed to be.

"Crenshaw, you said? You wouldn't be under any other name?"

Next to me, Marva puffs up.

"No, just that one. Are you *sure*?"

"Positive," he says, but he has the poll worker next to him check just in case. She shakes her head, too, after looking over it twice.

"Then he needs a provisional ballot," Marva says, stepping forward.

The man and woman behind the table exchange looks, but I can tell they're not up to arguing with Marva about her tone. She's not rude, exactly. Just...the type of serious that makes people question whether they really want to get into it with her.

"Okaaaaay," says the man. He shuffles around some

papers and slides a form across the table. "You just need to fill out this affidavit that confirms you're registered and legally allowed to vote."

Marva tugs on my sleeve, standing on her tiptoes. I lean down a bit to make it easier for her to whisper in my ear. "You're sure you're registered, right?"

"Yeah, I told you—"

"I *know* what you told me, but you never checked. You should check, just to make sure. If you're not registered, your vote won't count and this will all be for naught."

I snort. "Did you seriously just use the word *naught*?"

She sniffs. "Don't act like it's the first time you've heard it." Then she pulls out her phone and starts typing. After a few seconds, she hands it to me. "Here. Plug in your information. This site will tell you if you're registered."

I feel like I've been chosen to work out a complicated calculus problem in front of the class. Everyone within hearing distance is watching this go down. The people in line behind us are shifting impatiently, sighing and crossing and uncrossing their arms. The man and woman at the table are looking back and forth between Marva and me, no doubt wondering what she's going to do if my name doesn't come up on this site.

I say a silent prayer as I type in my info. Partly because

I'm wondering what Marva's going to do if I'm not registered. But also because . . . I really hope I am. I don't want to have dropped the ball on this. Sure, Marva seems to care more than most people I know, but she's not wrong. This shit is important.

You are not registered to vote.

Oh god.

I can't even say it. I just hand the phone back to her and look down at the floor.

"Okay," she says in a low voice. Lower than I've heard her sound all day. "Okay." She turns to the table again. "So, it turns out he's *not* registered. Can he do same-day registration?"

"Wait, what?" I stare at Marva, then the poll worker. "You can do that?"

"Absolutely," the man says. "Not every state has it yet, but you're in luck, because we do—as of last year. We'll just need to see your ID, and that counts as proof of residency if the address is current."

I grab my wallet and pull out my driver's license and—

"Christ."

Marva's face falls even further. "What."

She's so frustrated it's not even a question.

"This...It has my mom's address," I say, waving my ID. "Where I live. So—"

She blows out a stream of air. "So we have to go back to the other polling place."

"I'm so sorry," I mutter. I don't know if it's to Marva or the poll workers or the whole room. Maybe it's to the world, to apologize for my shitty existence. Why can't I do anything right?

"Good luck," says the man, looking from me to Marva and back to me again.

I nod and follow Marva out of the parent center, not making eye contact with anyone.

She's walking so fast and I'm so busy trying to figure out how pissed she's going to be that I'm not paying attention to anything around me. Or anyone.

"Duke."

I close my eyes, half hoping it's Ms. Amster again. But I know better than that. Because I'd know *this* voice anywhere.

I open my eyes and turn around. "Hey, Ma."

MARVA

I'M HALFWAY TO THE FRONT DOORS WHEN I REALIZE Duke isn't shuffling along behind me.

But before I can turn around, my phone buzzes. I whip it out of my pocket and quickly pull up new texts from my dad:

Still no Selma, but Mr. Lehman thinks he saw her in his backyard earlier

I'm looking, honey

More soon

I type back a quick thanks. I feel sick. Mr. Lehman lives at the end of the cul-de-sac, which means Selma has probably crossed over to another street by now. Does she even know how to cross the street without getting hit? Does she even know Dad's voice? I swallow.

And I really need Duke to hurry up so we can get to the church. I briefly thought about going back to school for the afternoon, but I don't think I'd be able to concentrate on anything with Selma missing and all this voting drama.

When I turn to look for him, I see he's standing a few feet outside the parent center. His back is to me, and he's so tall I can't tell who he's talking to. Maybe that woman from earlier? I decide to head over there. If she's still giving him shit about missing school, he's going to need backup.

But as I get closer, I see it's not the same person at all. This woman is also white, but she has a blond bob and she's tall. Not as tall as Duke, but he doesn't tower over her like he does me and most people. And she looks angry.

I'm too close by the time I realize it's probably his mother. She sees me watching them, and at first, her lips don't stop moving. But then, when I don't move away quickly enough, she stops talking and stares.

Duke turns around and gives me a look. I can't quite read it, but I'm pretty sure he doesn't want me here right now. Too late.

"Uh, Ma, this is Marva. The girl I was telling you about. She's been helping me vote. Or try to vote."

"Hello," I say, stepping forward with my hand out. "I'm Marva Sheridan."

Duke's mother appraises me for what seems like hours. Finally, she gives me a quick, firm handshake. "Hello, Marva. Duke tells me you've been driving him all around this morning."

"Yes, his car broke down, so I offered. I've been working hard to get people to vote for the last two years, so . . ."

"And it's all right with your parents that you're not in school right now?"

"They appreciate my efforts to get everyone involved in the election."

His mother narrows her eyes for a moment, then gives me a small smile. "A woman after my own heart. If you don't mind, I need to speak with Duke for a few more minutes."

"Of course," I say. Then, to Duke: "I'll wait for you out front."

"Nice to meet you, Marva," says his mother. "Thank you for helping my son."

"Nice meeting you, too," I say. "And it's my pleasure."

It's my pleasure? My neck burns as I turn away from

them. When I'm pretty sure they aren't still looking at me, I power-walk to the front doors as fast as I can.

Sitting outside on a bench, I pull up the Eartha Kitty account and scroll aimlessly through the pictures. I'm a little embarrassed that I've taken such pains to keep this whole thing a secret. I'm not ashamed of Eartha Kitty, I just don't think people would understand why I'm doing it. I'm the last person anyone would expect to have a page devoted to cute animals. Every time I see an account like this I assume it's some silly fifth-grader or someone my parents' age with way too much time on their hands. What if a college admissions board found out and thought I wasn't a desirable candidate for their program?

Tears prick at the corners of my eyes, and I start to brush them away at first, but then I think, *Who the hell cares?* My cat is missing and I love her and I want her back. Besides, is there a more appropriate place to cry than an elementary school? I bet not a day goes by here where someone doesn't get caught bawling.

Alec is the only one who knows about Selma's alter ego. I wonder if I should tell him that she ran away. Except I remember I never texted him back. I pull up our text chain, looking through our past messages.

Up until he texted last night, you wouldn't even know

we'd disagreed about colleges or voting, because we never discussed either in writing. Anyone looking at our messages would think everything was perfect between us. It was all making plans for dinners and movies and studying. Texting each other good night and good morning. Him checking if my mom's bronchitis had cleared up, and me asking how his grandparents were doing up in Pearl Creek.

My eyes keep sliding back down to his last text, though.

Where are you?

I think about texting back right now, letting him know everything that's going on. He's still my boyfriend, and checking in is what we do if we haven't seen each other in a while. But he hasn't followed up, so does he really even care where I am? He's probably glad I'm not at school, reminding him of what an utter jackass he's being about this election.

More texts come through from Dad.

Got another lead

Heading over to the park

I close my eyes. The park? That seems so big. Too big for my sheltered little Selma. I swipe back to her pictures, letting a tear fall as my eyes open and land on the one of her from Valentine's Day. I think it's a bullshit commercialization of love, but Alec is into it. Like, getting-me-two-dozen-roses-and-taking-me-to-the-nicest-restaurant-in-town into it. So, for our second Valentine's Day together, I decided to get Selma in on the action. I posed her with roses (that she immediately tried to eat) and a satin red heart (ditto) and took a bunch of photos with the Valentine's Day filter, which made it look like hearts were bursting out of her sweet little head.

What if Election Day is the last holiday I get to celebrate with her? What if she's—

"Hey, sorry about that," Duke says, standing over me. His tall form casts a long shadow across me and the bench.

"How mad is she?" I ask, swiping a finger under my eyes.

He shrugs. "Pretty pissed. But not about me missing school to vote. She's actually okay with that, except that I didn't tell her I was coming here. She didn't like having to hear it from Ms. Amster."

"So what is she mad about?"

"My sister..." He shakes his head. "It's a long story."

I nod, and when it's clear he's not going to expound on that, I say, "Well, should we head back to the church?"

"Yeah, I guess...."

But he doesn't sound so excited about it. And, truthfully, I'm not either. I want us to get there eventually. And we will, now that we know where he's supposed to be and what he has to do to get that vote in. But right now, all I can think about is—

"Would you mind if we go back to my house and maybe look around a bit for my cat? I just can't stop thinking about her. She'll know my voice better than my dad's, and I—"

"Marva." His voice is so soft I'm worried my tears are going to come back if he keeps talking that way. "Of course we can go look for your cat. You've been driving my ass around all morning, even though this is all my fault. The least I can do is help you look for her."

"You don't have to help me, but I just—"

"You helped me. Now it's my turn to help you. Come on," he says, holding out his hand.

I hesitate for only a moment before I take it and stand.

DUKE

I FIGURED SHE'D DRIVE EVEN MORE LIKE A BAT out of hell now that there's an actual emergency, but Marva pulls out of the school parking lot at a normal speed. She tugs on the pink braid so much, I wonder if it's going to tear right out of her head. I don't know what to say, so I keep quiet. And ignore how Ma said *We have a lot to talk about later.*

Marva lives pretty close to me, which kind of freaks me out. Yeah, we were at the same polling place, but it's weird to think of her living just a mile away all this time.

Have I seen her before? I glance over. Nah, I'm *sure* I'd remember her.

Marva turns into a cul-de-sac, slows down, and parks in front of a two-story gray house with white shutters. The outside looks like a home-and-garden magazine, with boxes of flowers under the windows and rosebushes by the porch. It's not as big as our house, but it is bigger than the one we had in our old town. Our house seems too big now that it's just me, Ma, and Ida. Sometimes I hear Ma pacing around at night, her house slippers scuffing down the hardwood floors like she has somewhere to be. Over and over again. She used to pace like that when she knew Julian was at a protest that had gotten out of hand.

"Want me to wait out here?" I ask just before Marva jumps out of the car. She almost forgot to take off her seat belt.

I can see her thinking through that scenario. There's a car in the driveway, so her dad is probably still here. How is she going to explain me? Ma and Dad were used to strange people being in our house all the time when Julian was around, because his apartment was too small for meetings. But I don't know about other people's parents.

"No, come in. It's just my dad."

I slip my sticks in my back pocket before I get out and follow her up the path. She moves fast. She's already inside before I make it to the porch. She leaves the door open and I hustle up the steps to catch up with her.

When I get inside, she's calling out, "Dad? Are you back? Did you find her?"

"In the kitchen, honey!" a voice calls.

Her dad is standing by the sink with his shirtsleeves rolled up, drinking a glass of water. The kitchen is bright yellow with a fruit bowl full of lemons on the counter and tons of pictures and papers stuck to the fridge door.

Marva's shoulders sag as she stands in the doorway, looking at him. "You didn't find her."

"I didn't." He rubs his eyes, closing them for a few moments. "I'm so sorry, Marva."

"It's okay. I know you didn't do it on purpose. She's never even *looked* like she wanted to go out before. I don't get it."

When her dad opens his eyes, he stares at me and jumps a little, like he's just now registered I'm standing behind her. That's new. Normally I'm the first person people notice. "Who are you?"

Marva sighs and waves her arm in my general direction. "This is Duke."

"Duke?" he repeats, like he needs to sit with it for a minute.

"Duke Crenshaw," I say, nodding. "Nice to meet you."

He squints at me. "Do you go to Salinas Prep?"

"No . . . Flores Hills High." I crack my knuckles at my side. Is Marva going to explain what's going on before he freaks out about why I'm standing in his kitchen in the middle of a school day?

"Ah," he says, nodding back at me. "Didn't think I'd seen any brothers around Salinas."

"Dad, this isn't really the time for small talk," Marva says, and she sounds like she's near tears. I *think* she was crying earlier, when I found her on the bench outside, but I'm pretty sure she didn't want me to see that.

Her dad's face changes and I know that look: *Please don't cry in front of me, because I don't know what to do*. He runs a hand over his chin and says, "It's going to be okay, Marva. Selma has a great life. She probably just wants to see what's out there and she'll come right back."

"We still have to keep looking for her," she says in that choked voice, and I wonder if she's actually crying now.

"I know, honey. Of course we do." He walks over to her, wraps her in his arms, and rubs her shaking back. "Of course."

My phone buzzes. Feels rude to pick it up here when Marva is so upset, so when it's clear her dad has this whole "comforting" thing covered, I duck into the attached dining room to see who's texted.

It's *my* dad. And after what Ma told me today, I'm pretty sure he's not texting just to say what's up.

I open the message quickly, like ripping off a Band-Aid to minimize the pain. And . . . yeah, he's pissed.

I know about your sister's little incident

And I know you had something to do with it

Man, today is not my day.

ABOUT IDA.

I'VE NEVER REALLY FELT LIKE THE MIDDLE KID. Since there's such a big age gap between Julian and Ida, I've always felt like Ida's big brother and Julian's little bro. But never the middle.

Julian was out of the house by the time he was eighteen. Ida was only eight when he moved out, and even though he was still there a lot, she didn't spend much time with him. He was usually holding meetings or on the phone or jumping up from the dinner table before we were done because he was always double-booking.

When he died, Ida said she felt bad, like she should be

more upset than she was. "But I didn't know him," she whispered to me as we sat on the porch of our old house, watching people leave the repast. "He was like a stranger. I . . . I love him, and what happened to him makes me sad, but I don't think I feel like the rest of you do."

I looked at her. She blinked back at me. Then I put my arm around her because even if I didn't understand what she was feeling, it couldn't have been easy to say something like that.

Ida and I aren't best friends or anything, but we talk sometimes. We have different groups of friends. I hang with the musicians and stoners, and she kicks it with the activists at FHH. Which is funny because she didn't really know Julian, but she's following in his footsteps. And Ma hates it.

They got in a big fight at dinner a couple months ago, when Ida announced she was going to a protest that weekend with the social justice club.

"No, you're not," Ma said as she took a bite of chicken and rice. She didn't even look up.

Ida glanced at me and cleared her throat. "Ma, come on. It's just a protest. Julian went to those all the time."

"You are not Julian. You are my little girl, and you're not going."

"I'm not a little girl," Ida grumbled. She stabbed at her plate so hard I was sure she'd break through it with her fork.

A few weeks ago, as soon as we got in the car for school, she said, "I need you to do something for me."

I was suspicious right away. Not because she asks for stuff all the time, but because she *doesn't*. Ida may be three years younger than me, but she's more independent than most people I know. She'd do everything herself if she could.

"What's up?" I asked, glancing in the rearview mirror before I pulled out of the driveway.

"I'm going to a protest this weekend, and I need you to drive me and pick me up."

"You can't get a ride from someone in the club?"

She swallowed. "It's not an official club event. Just some of us going on our own, and so I need a ride."

"Come on, Ida. You know Ma and Dad don't like you going to those things."

"*Those things?*" She crossed her arms. "Okay, first of all, you didn't even ask what the protest is for."

I stopped the car at the end of the driveway. I don't like her yapping in my ear on a normal day, but it seemed like this was something I actually needed to listen to.

"What's the protest for, Ida?"

"We're sitting in at Congressman Haywood's office to oppose his stance on abortion."

"Ida." I paused. "You sure you want to get involved in that?"

"He's *anti-choice*, Duke. He wants women to carry babies to term, like, no matter what. He doesn't care if they're sick or the baby is sick or if it's just not something they want to do! Do you think it's okay that some old man is trying to legislate what women choose to do with their own bodies?"

I shrugged, my hands back on the steering wheel. The car was still idling at the end of the driveway.

"What does that mean? Either you do or you don't think it's okay. Spit it out, big brother."

"I mean, I don't think women should have to have babies if it's going to kill them," I said. "Or if they're, uh, forced to do things against their will..."

Ida sighed. "Rape. The word is *rape*. You can say it, you know."

I swallowed hard. Ida always spoke her mind, but I wasn't sure I'd ever get used to my little sister schooling me like that.

"O-*kay*, I don't think women should have to have a

baby if they're raped either." I coughed, already knowing I shouldn't say what I was going to say but going through with it anyway. I'm good at that. "But I dunno. I guess... I don't really believe in it for other situations."

Ida let out a sharp laugh. "You don't *believe* in it? News flash: *It* still happens. All over the world. Legal or not. And anyway, why should I give a shit about what you think?"

My eyes got big.

"I mean, I do, Duke. You're my brother. I respect you." She paused. "But you don't have a uterus. And you don't know what it's like to be a woman. So, no offense, but if you're going to spend the whole day judging me, I'll just find another ride."

Damn. She was right. I didn't know what it was like. And I guess I hadn't thought much about it before. I've never even had sex, so that kind of stuff always seemed like it wasn't my problem.

Maybe this was one of those times I should just shut up and help my sister.

"So you need a ride there and back?" I mumbled, staring at the dusty dashboard.

"Yeah, and... well, it's an act of civil disobedience, so..."

I blew out a whoosh of air. "So there's a chance you could get arrested."

Julian was no stranger to that.

She nodded.

"You sure you don't want to tell Ma? Have her go with you?" I thought she might take it better than our dad. Maybe.

"No," Ida said firmly. "And you'd better not either. You're eighteen, Duke. An adult. You have all the same rights as Ma and Dad."

That didn't mean I had any idea what I was doing. Most of the time I felt like Ida had her shit together more than me. But all I said was, "Okay. I got you."

"Yeah?" She looked at me with wide, hopeful eyes. Like I was her goddamn hero or something. Little sisters, man...

"Yeah."

She sat back in her seat with a big, dopey smile. "Thanks, big brother."

I looked away. Put the car into reverse again, swinging out of the driveway before I glanced at her and said, "Fine. But if they ever find out, I'll deny everything."

MARVA

I CAN'T REMEMBER THE LAST TIME I CRIED IN front of anyone, and I feel foolish as soon as the sobs let up enough for me to breathe. Squeezing out a couple of tears in front of the elementary school was one thing, but this? When I pull away from Dad's arms, the shoulder of his shirt is soaked.

"Sorry," I mutter, grabbing a paper towel from the roll on the counter. I wipe my eyes and cheeks with it before tossing it into the trash can.

"Honey, *I'm* sorry," Dad says, and he looks it, even beneath the tired dark bags gathered under his eyes.

"Truly. Should we split up and try to find her? I'm game to go back out again."

"Yes, I was thinking that Duke and I could—" I turn around to face him, even though I'm beyond embarrassed that he witnessed my crying. Except he's not there.

He's in the dining room, pacing back and forth. He stops for a moment, framed in the doorway, staring silently at his phone.

I turn back to my father, who's looking at him curiously. "How do you two know each other again?"

"Just... from around the neighborhood," I say, thinking about how we were registered at the same polling place. Or how he was *supposed* to be registered there. "I think we should figure out a plan for the search party."

It may be generous calling three people a search party, but it's better than just Dad or me. I whip out my phone and pull up the maps app so my dad won't be tempted to ask more questions, like why I was able to get out of school and back home so quickly.

Duke walks slowly into the kitchen a couple of minutes later, wearing a look I don't quite recognize. It's not good, whatever it is.

"Everything okay?" I ask as he walks over to stand near me.

He gives me a weak smile. "You ready to look for this cat?"

And we do. We look *everywhere* for Selma.

Dad takes the area west of French Street, and Duke and I head in the opposite direction, turning right out of the cul-de-sac by the Lehmans'. Together. The neighbors know Dad and me, but *I* know how people are in this neighborhood when they see a strange Black person walking around, as if we don't have the right to be everywhere white people are without a permit, so I think it's safer if Duke stays with me. He doesn't object.

"Has she ever run off before?" he asks when we've walked three blocks.

"Never," I say.

We're calling her name, looking under bushes, peering up at trees. I ask anyone we come across if they've seen a cat fitting her description, but everyone shakes their head, apologetic. After about twenty minutes, I pull up a photo of her to show people, making sure it's not one of the heavily posed ones from Selma's social media. Duke looks at it but doesn't seem to recognize her from the Eartha Kitty account. Thank god.

After an hour, I'm beginning to lose hope. And that makes me cranky. Giving up is not in my nature, which I think is pretty obvious to anyone who saw me canvassing for the election. But it's hot. And I'm hungry. And tired. And Duke and I still have to get back to the church so he can register.

Dad calls just as I start thinking about turning around. "I wish I had better news," he says, "but I haven't seen her, honey. Neither has anyone else. I think we might need to call it a day for now. Or an afternoon, at the very least."

"Okay," I say in a quiet voice.

Duke stands a few feet away, leaning against a tree. He's staring at a blue house across the street.

"Meet me back at the house and I'll make us all some lunch. That is, unless you have other plans?"

I think that's my dad's not-so-subtle way of hinting that he hasn't forgotten I'm supposed to be in school, but I play dumb and say we'll see him in a few.

I hang up and follow Duke's gaze. "Why are you looking at that house like that?"

"I think I know it. I mean, I was there not too long ago. . . ."

"How far away do you live from here?" I ask, suddenly

wondering if I *could* have known Duke from around the neighborhood all this time. But wouldn't I have noticed him? He's hard to miss... and not just because of his size. My neck is heating up and I'm annoyed with myself for daring to flush with embarrassment in a time of crisis.

"Just about three blocks that way," he says, pointing. "Drugstore Sorrow played a gig at this house."

"Bad gig?"

He's actually *grimacing*.

Duke shrugs and I don't press him. I've got Selma on the brain.

When we get back to my house, Dad is already home, puttering around in the kitchen. He does most of the cooking since he keeps more regular hours than Mom. I think he likes it, though. I never hear him hum except for when he's in the kitchen, and lately, he's taken to dancing around, especially when he's making his favorite dishes. Normally I'd be embarrassed that Duke is witnessing this, but I'm too tired to care.

I set out plates while Dad makes fried bologna sandwiches. It's not a coincidence. They're my favorite sandwich, so he usually makes them when I need cheering up. Like the time I got a C+ on my chemistry test, even though

I'd studied for weeks beforehand. Or when I got passed over for the internship at the mayor's office last summer. I ate a lot of bologna sandwiches my freshman year.

I remember the first time we made them for Alec. He was horrified at first—"You *fry bologna*?"—but as soon as he had his first bite, he was asking for another sandwich.

"We can only get away with this when Marva's mom isn't home. She loves them but says that doesn't outweigh how unhealthy they are," Dad says, sliding plates in front of Duke and me.

He squeezes my shoulder before he goes back to the stove. "And they're only to be eaten with wads of paper towels, not fancy napkins."

"I've never had one," Duke says. He pulls his drumsticks out of his back pocket and sets them on the table next to his plate. I wonder why he carries them with him when they could've stayed in his backpack. Are they like a security blanket?

Dad's head whips around to stare at him as he throws another piece of bologna into the skillet and cuts a slit in the middle. "For real?"

"Yeah, I don't think my mom's ever bought bologna, and my dad's on a steady diet of takeout since the divorce."

He snaps his mouth closed like he's said too much, but I kind of want him to keep going. That talk with his mom didn't look so good.

"Well, I *lived* on these at Morehouse," my dad says. "I could eat for a whole week for less than ten dollars."

"You went to Morehouse?" Duke is sitting with his hands in his lap, waiting for Dad to come to the table.

I pick up my sandwich and nod toward his plate. "You don't have to wait. We're not that formal."

"Better eat it while it's hot," Dad offers from the stove, flipping over the slices of popping bologna. "And yup, class of 1992. One of the best decisions I've ever made. Are you headed off to college next year like Marva?"

"I am." Duke picks up his sandwich. I watch as he takes a giant bite, and it's worth it to see how his face changes. From neutral to surprise to pure bliss, which I'm pretty sure was exactly how I felt the first time I had one of these. "Damn, this— I mean, this is really good, Mr. Sheridan."

"Call me Terrell," Dad says right away.

"Honestly, Terrell, I think I might be falling in love," Duke says, swallowing after his second bite. "This is one of the best things I've ever eaten."

"Glad you like it. And I hope you're applying to my

alma mater? Think you'd be a good Morehouse man, Duke."

Duke sets down his sandwich and wipes his hands on the paper towel next to his plate. "I know about Morehouse, but... I don't know where I'm applying yet."

I raise my eyebrows. Alec and I haven't had an easy time agreeing on the same schools, but I've known where I want to apply since freshman year. It's hard to believe not everyone has had it planned out for so long, too. Though, the more I get to know Duke, the less it surprises me the way he does things. We're complete opposites. In almost everything, it seems.

"Well, if you ever want to talk to anyone about it, I'm happy to help." Dad turns off the burner and moves the skillet to a cool one, assembles his sandwich, and joins us at the table, where Duke and I are both halfway done with ours.

I guess I wasn't the only one who'd worked up an appetite. It's barely past noon, but it's already been a day.

"Marva, I was thinking," Dad says as he sits down next to me at the round table, "maybe you could post something about Selma on her account."

If I could get away with it, I would totally kick him under the table right now.

Duke looks back and forth between us. "What account?"

Honestly, parents are not to be trusted with secrets.

The Eartha Kitty account wasn't a big deal at first. Everyone who's ever met Selma has commented on how beautiful she is—even ardent non-cat people, who love nothing more than to tell you how much they are *not* into cats—so I thought she might get a few likes here and there when she was being particularly cute. But then other pet accounts started following and liking and reposting her photos, and she started getting a *real* following. Like, actual strangers and not just people who knew her in real life. And people from Salinas Prep, who had no idea I was the one behind the account.

Then, like anything else I'm involved with, I started to take it seriously. I have a schedule for new content, which I set up to post in the future, always at the same time of day. I started coordinating Eartha Kitty's posts with holidays and current events. And *then*, when the election campaigns began, I decided Eartha Kitty might as well help get the word out about voting. It turns out people love political posts involving cats, and her following grew by the thousands. I'm up to almost four hundred thousand. And I'm constantly combing through emails for sponsorship requests, trying to figure out which ones to entertain. I felt weird about it at first. Unethical. Selma didn't ask for any of this. But the money was too good to pass up. Mom and Dad are already paying enough for my education at Salinas Prep—the least I can do is help out with my college tuition.

But the more famous Selma's alter ego became, the more nervous I got about anyone knowing. I want to be known as Marva Sheridan, aspiring attorney, not the girl who posts cutely staged cat photos for the masses. I'm student council president and in the running for valedictorian; I want to be known for my academic and civic accomplishments, not my social media skills. I finally told Alec, but only because he once stopped by unexpectedly and caught us in the middle of a photo shoot. I know for sure he hasn't told anyone; nothing stays secret for long once it gets out at Salinas Prep. Your run-of-the-mill gossip about a crush can make it through the entire student body by fifth period.

"You haven't told him about Eartha Kitty?" Dad asks, taking a big bite of his sandwich. Mustard squirts out onto his shirt, and I think it serves him right for making me explain this to Duke.

To be fair, Dad was the one who suggested her internet name. I laughed at first, because all I knew about Eartha

Kitt the woman was that she had been a singer, played Catwoman a long time ago, and was considered a sex symbol. But Dad told me she'd done a lot of good, so I looked her up and was shocked to see *how much* she'd done. Why was she not also known for how she helped out underprivileged kids and spoke out against the Vietnam War and advocated for LGBTQ rights? She was even under CIA surveillance at one point because of her political views, but instead of being embarrassed, she told the *New York Times* they could print parts of her file and apparently said, "I have nothing to be afraid of and I have nothing to hide." She was a total badass.

And I guess... well, Eartha Kitt the woman gave me courage. If she could be a sex symbol *and* politically involved, why couldn't I be a serious student and also have a social media account for my cat?

At least, it made sense back then. Now... as I look at Duke, I wish I could disappear under the table.

His eyes widen like slices of bologna when he puts two and two together. "Wait. Your cat... that's missing... is Eartha Kitty? *The* Eartha Kitty?"

"Mm-hmm," I say, keeping my eyes on my plate.

He hoots. "You have, like, half a million followers! Man, Ida is gonna be obsessed with you."

My neck is burning so hot I think my braids might catch on fire. I shake my head. "It's not a big deal."

"She's for sure a big deal. Ida said people have written articles about her."

"Well, I don't care about any of that. The Eartha Kitty stuff. I just want my cat back. *Selma*," I say, finally looking at him. I don't know what I thought I'd find when I met his eyes. Maybe a smirk or barely concealed laughter. He said earlier that he's not into cats. What if he thinks it's silly that I care so much?

But he's nice. Nicer than he has any business being, considering he spent an hour in the blazing sun helping me look for her and is now sitting at a strange table eating sandwiches with two strange people.

That niceness is reflected in his eyes. And his voice, when he says, "I know. I'm sorry. She'll come back, okay? You treat her too good for her to go anywhere else."

And I don't know why I feel so comforted by his words when my father has been saying the same thing since he called to tell me the bad news. But dads are *supposed* to comfort you. It's part of the job. Like knowing when to make my favorite sandwich. Duke doesn't owe me anything. He's only known me a few hours.

"And maybe . . ." He exchanges a look with my father

like they're old friends. I don't like it. "Maybe you *should* post that she's missing. Who knows her better than her fans? You could get a ton of people looking for her, which is way more than what we could do."

He's not wrong. But then I'd have to reveal our neighborhood, which seems too risky. And it would be like breaking the fourth wall, admitting that Selma is still a regular cat who does regular things, like try to run away. Part of the attraction is the illusion of her being perfect and almost an otherworldly feline.

"I'll think about it," I finally say so they'll stop looking at me.

DUKE

I WISH MY DAD WERE AS CHILL AS MARVA'S.

As we finish up our sandwiches, he asks about my drumsticks. I don't tell him that I started drumming for therapy and now I can't imagine my life without it. Or that keeping my sticks with me is the fastest way to get rid of anxiety when it ratchets up so high I feel like I can't breathe.

I do tell him Drugstore Sorrow has its first paying gig tonight. He smiles real big and says, "All right now. You doing the thing, Duke."

"Trying to," I say, my head dipping low as I run my knuckles over the sticks. I don't think my dad's ever been proud of anything I've done. Or if he has, he's never said so. Not like Ma, who makes sure to tell us when we're doing good, same as when we're screwing up.

He wasn't always like this, my dad. He wasn't always so irritated and impatient, and his temper wasn't always so quick. A lot of things changed after my brother died, but I think my dad might be the biggest change of all.

Marva pops the last bite of sandwich in her mouth, wipes her lips with a paper towel, and says, "We need to hit the road. The lines are only going to get longer the more we wait."

"Where you headed?" asks her dad as he scoops up our plates and takes them to the sink before I can get up to help.

"To the church, so he can vote." Marva stares at him. "Have *you* voted today?"

"Yes, I stopped by on my way home from the airport because I knew you'd ask." He pauses, nodding at the sticker on her shirt. "But you've already voted. Was this before or after Mrs. Thomas saw you at Drip Drop?"

Marva's mouth drops open. "I *knew* it," she mutters. "Listen, it's been a weird morning, Dad. But I swear, I'm not just skipping school for fun. Duke's been having problems at the polls and—"

"Honey, it's fine," he says, his mouth turning up in a smile. "Sheila needs to get a grip and worry about her own kids. Do you think I don't know you wouldn't cut school for fun? In fact, maybe you *should* cut school for fun sometime. Just to remind me you're still a teenager?"

"Yeah, sure, Dad. Thanks for lunch." She kisses his cheek, then says, "Maybe you should leave the door open for Selma . . . or a treat on the porch or something?"

He shakes his head. "I've seen raccoons out during the day here. I don't play with those monsters. I'm working from home the rest of the day, and I will let you know the second her paw crosses the porch steps." He turns to look at me. "Duke, a pleasure. You're welcome back anytime. And don't forget about Morehouse."

My heart jumps just like it did the first time he said it. Morehouse is another reminder of Julian. He got in, a full scholarship and everything. It was his first choice. And I thought Dad was going to kill him when he said he was staying home instead to take classes at the local college so he could do work in the community.

"Thanks, Terrell," I say as we dap each other up. "I won't."

On the way to the church, Marva drives the Volvo slowly down the side streets as she hangs her head out of the window, watching for Selma the whole way.

I look over when we pass the blue house again. That was a good gig. One of our best. It was a good night, until what happened with Kendall.

I don't really drink a lot, but I was nervous that night. It was the biggest gig we'd booked so far. Svetlana's cousin, who's a year younger than us but knows more people at FHH than the whole band combined, was having a party and asked if we wanted to play. Svetlana signed us up without asking, which breaks, like, our number-one rule. We're supposed to bring any opportunities to Kendall, since she's our manager, and then we all talk it through before we commit. But we all got over it pretty quick. It's not like we were gonna turn down the chance to play in front of actual people.

Very drunk people... but people. Anthony said we'd play better if we were sober, so I didn't have a drink until after the gig. By then, people were actually stumbling over their own feet and passing out on couches and stinking up the bathroom with puke.

I didn't do any of that. But I parked myself in the corner of the kitchen with Kendall and we claimed a bottle of cheap vodka and . . . I cringe as I think of that part of the night.

"I seriously can't believe how good the group is," Kendall said, reaching for the vodka for the second—no, third? Fourth?—time.

I held her blue plastic cup steady as she splashed more in. "What do you mean? You were, like, our only fan for a *minute*."

She laughed, slamming the bottle back down on the counter. Neither of us was wasted, but we were in that phase of drinking where everything is funny for some reason. I'd never gotten drunk with Kendall, and it was fun. *She* was fun. Which wasn't a surprise. I had known her before she started helping out with Drugstore Sorrow, but she acted like being our manager was a job that paid her in more than a few thank-yous from the group and the occasional pizza after practice.

"Exactly, Duke," she said, shaking her head. "You guys have come a long way. A *loooooong* way."

I shook my head, slurping down more vodka and club soda as she cackled again.

Then, suddenly, her face changed. And maybe I should've seen it coming, but everything was a little hazy and we'd just played like an actual band and I was happy.

I still thought about Julian, but his death and wondering who shot him and why nobody cared to find out who had done it didn't haunt me every second of every day.

Kendall moved closer to me. There was barely a foot of space between us. "Do you ever dream about your brother?"

The question was a shock down my spine. Julian's death wasn't a secret, but I didn't talk to many people about it at FHH. Definitely not anyone besides her and the band. And the band only knew because we spent so much time together, not because I felt better when I talked to them about it.

I looked around the kitchen. We were the only ones on this side of the room, and no one was listening, but still. It felt like a marquee had just lit up over our heads, announcing that a meeting of the Dead Brothers Club had come to order.

"Uh, not really," I said, swigging from my drink. The room was starting to spin, but if she was going to bring this up—now, here—I needed something to help me deal.

"I had one. A dream last night. About Ethan." She blinked at me, and her brown eyes were watery and I wasn't sure if she was crying or if it was the vodka and...

damn. I didn't want to be there, and it made me feel bad because Kendall had been there for me. So many times.

"Oh yeah?" I tried to sound chill, but beads of sweat were popping up on my forehead, and I really, really hoped she wasn't going to go *there*.

"Yeah, he was . . . exactly the same as he was before he died. Still being annoying as hell, still eating up all the food in the house. But . . ." She stopped, brushing her bangs out of her eyes. Then she swallowed and said, "But he was still dead. The gunshot wounds were . . ."

I blew out a loud breath. "Damn."

"Yeah. It was like a dream and a nightmare all at once. To see him again, to be able to talk to him, but he was—"

Those were for sure tears in her eyes. I took another drink.

"You haven't had dreams about him?" she pressed, stepping even closer to me. "Julian?"

Kendall smelled so good, like flowers or something fresh. She looked good, too. Before I met her, I'd wondered if she'd look anything like the picture she'd sent me if I ever saw her in person. She looked exactly the same. Better, even.

I glanced around the kitchen again. Nobody was paying

attention to us. Some music was playing in the living room and it sounded like Anthony was messing around, freestyling on one of the mics. People were only stopping through the kitchen to get more to drink, not listen to us.

But I felt weird about it, this conversation. I think I would've felt weird no matter where we were having it.

"No," I said, even though that wasn't true. I'd had lots of dreams about my brother. But I talked to my therapist about that stuff. Not Kendall. I'd already told her so much online and over text, and honestly, the more I got to know her in person, the weirder I felt about how much she knew.

"Oh," she said. Her eyes moved down to her cup before she looked at me again. "Okay."

"Sorry," I said. "I just . . . Do you ever think it was better when we only knew each other online?"

That was the second to last time she looked me in the eye.

Now, in Marva's car, I slip my phone out of my pocket. Maybe I should text Kendall. Try one more time.

"Hey, is everything okay?" Marva nods toward my phone. "You looked kind of upset earlier. I'm not trying to pry, but—"

"It's all right," I say quickly. "Your dad cooked me lunch. Only fair if you know about my family, huh? And nah . . . everything's not okay. Not really. My parents are pretty pissed at me and my sister. Especially my dad. I kind of helped her do something that I knew would make him and my mom flip their shit if they found out. And they did."

I don't want to say more. Not because Ida's ashamed. She took the risk because of something she believes in. It's just not my story to tell, even though I was right there to bail her out and drive her home, where we had dinner with Ma, like nothing out of the ordinary had happened. The police didn't call Ma or Dad because I'm eighteen and I had the money to get her out. I figured she'd tell them before they heard, but she's good at keeping secrets, just like Julian was. Good at knowing when to upset our parents and when to keep her mouth shut. But, apparently, my sister, who is usually super smart about things, didn't think about the fact that her arrest record was public and someone we know might see it and tell our parents.

I've been texting Ida since I talked to Ma, but she's not responding. She didn't answer her phone when I tried to call either.

"Are you scared of your dad?" Marva asks, turning on her right blinker to switch lanes.

"Nah. He didn't use to yell like this when my brother

was around. I think . . ." I pause. Debate whether I should get into this. People get real curious about dead family members. Especially when they died young.

Marva looks over, waiting.

"I think he blames himself for Julian's death."

And that it was harder on him than he'll ever admit. Sometimes, the way he looks at me, I wonder if he wishes it had been me instead of Julian. I wonder that with both my parents, even though Ma hides it better.

"What happened?" she asks. Her voice is soft and curious, not demanding.

I swallow. It's been a minute since I've talked about this. People found out pretty quickly after we moved to Flores Hills, even though I did my best not to bring it up. But after the first few months, nobody mentioned it. Like I had a Dead Brother stamp on me that other people could see, but nobody wanted to know how it felt to be branded.

"He was shot. In a drive-by."

"Oh," Marva says. "Oh. I'm so sorry, Duke."

"It's okay."

"It's really not," she says.

I'm so used to people having the wrong reaction that I can't believe it when I hear the right one. I can see the way people's whole perception of me changes when I tell them the way Julian died. It's not the same face they use when someone died from cancer. Then there are the others, who don't look surprised, like the only place they'd expect him to be by that age was dead or in prison.

"But why does your dad blame himself?"

"I don't really know. For letting him get so involved in activism? For daring to have a Black son?" I shrug. "You want to know the fucked-up thing? Julian was working on getting more attention on gun control in low-income areas. That was his big priority, since he said everyone wants to talk about Black-on-Black crime instead of the actual issues behind the crime."

"Exactly," Marva says in a passionate tone that sounds just like my brother. It still freaks me out how much she reminds me of him in some ways. "One of my boyfriend's friends tried to pull that Black-on-Black crime shit with me once and Alec almost murdered him."

"You didn't get to him first?"

"Surprisingly, no." She pauses. "I guess I'm glad Alec stepped up. I would've been pissed if he'd just let his friend get away with that."

"How is *that*?" I ask.

"What?"

"Dating a white guy," I say, echoing her question about

my mom earlier. Which for real seems like it was about a thousand years ago and not just this morning.

Marva pulls down the car's sun visor and sits up as straight as possible, but the sun is still shining right in her face. "I don't think about it a lot. Not all the time. Actually . . . part of the reason I got with him is because he was so involved in social justice. He stands up for the right thing, even if it's not the popular thing."

"Except when it comes to voting?"

"Well, nobody's perfect, right?"

But I'm not convinced. I think it's more than him not being perfect. I mean, I'm the last person who knows anything about relationships, but she tenses up every time she mentions him. That doesn't seem like something that should happen when you're really into someone.

"Yeah, but that's a big deal to you, right? Seems like he should be trying a little harder to keep you happy."

She stares out the windshield, gripping the steering wheel and saying nothing.

"Sorry," I say. "It's not my business."

She presses her lips together before she sighs and says, "You're not wrong." She clears her throat. "What about you? Haven't you ever dated girls who weren't Black?"

Define dating is what I want to say, but I just shrug. "Not really."

"Not really? Either you have or you haven't."

A driver cuts her off just before she's about to turn onto the street for the church. She swerves and throws them the finger, and I am saved from telling her exactly how inexperienced I am when it comes to girls.

And how, when I do get close to girls, I seem incapable of not fucking it up.

Her phone rings then, and she gestures to the console. "Could you grab that? It's probably my dad. Maybe he has a lead on Selma!"

I pick up her phone, barely glancing at the screen before I answer.

But milliseconds before my thumb hits the talk button, I see the name flashing across the screen.

Alec Buckman

Shiiiiiiiiiiit.

I don't like drama or confrontation. I'll do anything to avoid it, from making myself seem smaller when I know dudes are trying to mess with me to, well, handling things the way I did with Kendall. Some people might call it cowardly or a dick move, but I'm not looking for trouble.

So I'm not sure why I don't just tell her she needs to answer it. Or just send the call to voicemail. Or... anything besides what I do.

Which is pick up and say hello.

There's a long pause on the other end. So long I think he must have hung up. Then a deep voice says, "Uhhh, I'm trying to get ahold of Marva?"

I look at her and wonder if she's going to kill me while the car is still moving.

"What does he want? Is it about Selma? Tell him I'm driving!"

"She, ah, can't come to the phone right now. Can I have her call you back?"

"Who *is* this?"

"I think she might be able to explain better. Can she call you in a few?"

Marva frowns. "Is that my dad?"

"Sure," the voice says, tight and low. "Will you tell Marva that *Alec* called?"

MARVA

"I, AH, THINK THAT WAS YOUR BOYFRIEND." HE slides the phone into the console and sits back in his seat.

"*What?*" I squeeze my hands around the steering wheel so I won't go careening into the church parking lot. "That was *Alec*? Why did you answer?"

"You told me to—"

"Because I thought it was my *dad*. Jesus, Duke!"

He sighs. "Sorry. I…"

But he doesn't finish, so I have no clue why the hell he would think it was a good idea to answer the phone when my boyfriend was calling. God, I can't even imagine what

Alec is thinking right now. Especially since I never texted him back this morning.

"Do you mind if I call him after I park? I don't want him to—"

"Worry? I get it," he says easily. "I probably wouldn't like it if my girl were in the car with a strange dude."

I'm pretty sure Alec is leaning more toward pissed than worried. And I guess I'll find out soon enough.

Except I can't find a space. The parking lot of the church is enormous, and it's completely full now. Ugh. I drive around one more time, hoping to catch someone as they're leaving. But no one's coming out, and as I slowly drive past the entrance, I see the line is trailing out the door and all the way around the colossal stone building.

"Damn, this is wild," Duke says, craning his neck to look at the line.

I pull out of the lot and cruise down the local side streets, but they're packed, too. I finally squeeze into a spot a couple of blocks away and get out, clutching my phone.

We don't talk as we walk to the church. Duke's got his drumsticks out again, drumming on his thighs in the absence of another surface. He is totally lost in his rhythm, and I can't stop looking at my phone, thinking of Alec.

When we get to the church, I tell Duke I'll catch up to him. He goes to stand in line while I find a quiet spot around the side.

I pull up Alec's number in my list of favorites and lean against the building.

The phone rings three times before he picks up. I hold my breath, waiting for his voice.

"You got my message?" He doesn't sound mean, exactly, but definitely not happy.

He sounds . . . cold.

"I *know* this is going to seem ridiculous, but hear me out." I quickly explain my whole day, starting with showing up at the polling place and ending with two minutes ago. "This is probably the weirdest day I've ever had, and it's still not over."

Alec takes a deep breath, and I brace myself for the white-hot anger I'm sure is bubbling under the surface. Except—that's not what happens at all.

"Okay," he says, and then I hear someone calling his name. It sounds crowded, like he's walking around between classes.

"What are you doing?"

"Heading to Government," he says.

I practically laugh at the irony. But if his tone before was cold, it's cool now. Which is somehow even worse. Cold means he's *trying* to be unkind. Cool means indifference.

"Well, did you hear what I said? Selma is *missing*. She's been gone since before lunch. What if she never comes home?"

"She'll come home, Marva."

I hesitate. Something is off about this. About *him*. It's like I'm talking to a stranger. One who doesn't care much about what happens to me or my cat. And who doesn't care about me hanging out with some guy all day instead of texting him back.

"Do... Do you want to come help me look for her when you get out of school? I should be all finished helping Duke by then."

I said his name again on purpose, just to remind Alec that he should be upset. And I get... nothing.

"Text me when you're done," he says. "I'll try to meet up with you."

That one little word sets me off like a bomb.

"You'll *try*?" I have to stop myself from shouting. "Alec, I'm your *girlfriend*. You know how important Selma is to me. She's like family. And what else are you doing? It's not like you need to get somewhere to vote."

A long, thick silence blooms between us.

"Marva, I've already told you this is my choice." His voice is so eerily calm it enrages me further, though I didn't think that was possible. "You may not have been listening or believed me, but what I said stands. I'm not changing my mind. And you're not going to change me, so maybe you should just give up now."

My head jerks back. "*Give up?* On you voting? Or . . . ?"

I can't say it. Because the thought that Alec means I should give up on *us* makes my stomach cramp. Sure, things have been a little tense lately, and we haven't seemed to be on the same page like we usually are. But isn't that what happens when you've been in a relationship for a while? Don't you have to readjust? Go through rough patches to get to the good ones?

And we're Marva Sheridan and Alec Buckman: *the* couple at Salinas Prep. As soon as I became friends with Alec, everything turned around for me at school. I didn't act any differently than I had before, but I guess because I was Alec-approved, everyone felt comfortable actually getting to know me. Once we started dating, it was like people couldn't get enough of us.

"Maybe we should talk later," he says in that same cool voice.

"Yes, please. I mean, if you think you can make some time for me?" I can't keep the sarcasm from my voice.

"I'll hit you up after last period, okay?"

My throat is aching. And I don't know if I'm holding back tears because of Selma or Alec or how fucking frustrating it's been just trying to get *one* person's ballot in. Or if it's the worry I haven't been able to chase away for months now, despite my best efforts: What if this election doesn't go the way I and millions of other people want it—no, *need* it—to go?

It could be all three.

A text from him comes through not thirty seconds after we hang up. I swipe to open it. Maybe it's an apology, one he couldn't manage to say over the phone. Which I don't love, but it's better than nothing.

It's not an apology.

You should put up a missing poster for Selma on her page

ABOUT ALEC, PART 2.

ALEC AND I HAD BEEN FRIENDS FOR A LITTLE over six months when he asked me to come up to his grandparents' house.

It was late June, a couple of weeks after school had let out. We were at his house, eating a snack that Deena, the Buckmans' housekeeper, had made. He stood up to get us drinks.

"Hey, uh, do you want to go up to my grandparents' for the Fourth?" He was burning a path from the kitchen island to the professional-grade fridge, tossing the words over his shoulder.

He seemed nervous. And I wasn't sure I'd seen that before, but it was kind of cute. He was normally a ball of confidence wrapped up in disarming good looks, so it was kind of refreshing to see him flustered.

"Your grandparents?"

"Yeah, they live on a ranch north of here, and we go up every Fourth. I usually bring a friend, and this year I want it to be you."

I sat up straight on my stool, resting my hands on the cool marble countertop of the island. "Really?"

I don't know why I was so surprised. By then, Alec and I were spending a lot of time together. So much that people were starting to look at us strangely, as if they thought there was something more. I had to admit, once I'd gotten to know Alec, it had been easy to see why everyone couldn't stop talking about him. And I'd never needed much convincing on the attractive part.

But I really enjoyed his friendship. I loved talking to him in more detail about the causes we both followed online. He was passionate about lots of the same stuff I cared about: working toward a single-payer healthcare system, making sure immigrants are treated with empathy and humanity, putting an end to school shootings. Our conversations were so full of fire and good energy that I always left Alec feeling like I could change the world.

I knew Alec's parents by then, and they'd always been cool to me. But I have to say, I was a little skeptical about spending so much time with his grandparents—and on their turf. I'd encountered more than my fair share of my classmates' grandparents in vintage Chanel and Louis Vuitton who would smile in my face and question what I was doing at a place like Salinas Prep behind my back. Then there were the people who practically bragged about how racist their relatives were, nervous-laughing about how contentious holidays got when they brought up their differing politics.

Basically, I wasn't too excited about meeting the family of anyone who went to Salinas Prep, even Alec's. But I couldn't say that, because he was sweet to invite me. And he'd chosen me out of all his friends.

"Yes, really," he said, smiling. "Why not?"

"I don't know. . . . I mean, you have so many friends, I just didn't think . . ."

"Yeah, and you're one of my best," he said, walking over to stand in front of me. "Come to the ranch. You'll love it."

I stared into his soft gray eyes, and I didn't have the heart to tell him that celebrating July Fourth wasn't a priority for me. My parents and I had just celebrated Juneteenth with some of their friends—something I hadn't even mentioned to Alec because I had a strong feeling he didn't know what it was, and sometimes I got tired of explaining my Blackness.

"Yes," I said with a wide smile. "I mean, I have to check with my parents, but I'd love to. Thank you."

"Nana and Papa will be so stoked to meet you."

Wait. Did that mean he'd told his grandparents about me? But I shut down that tingling feeling right away. He probably told his grandparents about all his friends, and I was the newest.

By the time the trip rolled around a couple of weeks later, *I* was the nervous one. Mom sat on my bed while I packed, petting Selma and watching me.

"They're going to love you," she said.

"What if they don't? What if it's really awkward?"

"I can't imagine *anyone* not loving you, but if they don't, that's on them." Mom said it so simply. So matter-of-fact, as if no other possibility could exist.

But I'd never had an easy time making friends, and I

didn't see why this would be any different. Then again, I'd always been more comfortable around people older than me—like, my parents' age and up—so maybe being around Alec's grandparents wouldn't be so bad after all.

They lived in a town called Pearl Creek, and it was gorgeous. Quaint and filled with tiny specialized shops and historic buildings.

His grandparents lived on a sprawling lot that seemed to go on forever, with several smaller buildings set back from the main house on the rolling green hills. I instantly felt calmer the second we stepped out of the car. The air was clean and the land was quiet, and it felt as if we'd driven into some unknown paradise just hours from my home.

"We've heard so many wonderful things about you, Marva." Alec's grandmother embraced me as soon as I stepped foot on her porch. She smelled like lemons and rosemary, and when she pulled away, she looked right in my eyes and said, "But my grandson failed to tell me just how beautiful you are."

I glanced at Alec. He didn't object, and his face was turning the brightest shade of pink. I held back a giggle.

His grandfather was just as warm, hugging me as if

we'd known each other for years. "We're so happy you could make it, Marva. Alec tells us you're one of his best friends."

It didn't take me long to become smitten with them. Alec's nana and papa, who insisted I call them by their first names of Gertie and Frank, were two of the kindest people I'd ever met. They seemed genuinely interested in everything about me and asked a lot of questions—but not so many that it felt like they were being intrusive.

We got there late in the evening, so after a light meal of soup and salad, Gertie showed me to my room, all the way down the hall from Alec's. It had its own bathroom. And it was cozy, with fresh flowers in a vase on the table, soft linens on the bed, and a rocking chair in the corner.

"That used to be *my* grandmother's," Gertie said after she noticed me admiring it. "Somehow she got it all the way over here from Romania in the early twentieth century."

"It's beautiful," I said.

"Well, sleep tight, and let us know if you need anything, Marva. It's really wonderful having you here." She smiled before closing the door behind her.

The sweet smell of lavender wafting through the open window lulled me to sleep, and I woke up feeling more rested than I had all year. We headed down to the creek after breakfast, where we spent most of the day, then made a stop through town for a late lunch and to pick up any last things they'd forgotten for the Fourth the next day.

We all pitched in for dinner, which was shrimp salad, grilled haloumi with vegetables, prosciutto and mozzarella sandwiches, and the best lemonade I've ever had. This was the most time I'd ever spent with Alec's parents, and though they'd always been nice to me, they seemed even more relaxed up in Pearl Creek.

Gertie and Frank wouldn't let us help clean up ("Go be young and free," Frank said, holding up his glass of wine), so after we put our dishes in the sink, Alec asked if I wanted to take a walk around the land.

"What are all these buildings?" I pointed in the distance.

"Well, those are stables, even though the horses are long gone. That's an outhouse that's definitely not in use, and then there's a guesthouse where the ranch hands used to live back in the day."

We wandered out toward the guesthouse. Walking close enough for our elbows to bump together.

"When was the last time anyone lived here?" I asked, peering into the cloudy windows. As nice as his grandparents' house was, this looked like it hadn't been touched in years. The floorboards of the porch appeared as if they might rot through at any moment, the roof was sagging, and there was a giant rusted padlock on the front door.

"A long-ass time ago," Alec said, shrugging. "Maybe decades."

There wasn't much beyond that, but we walked. The sun was setting, and the sky was a brilliant pinky-orange. I don't pay much attention to sunsets; personally, I think people post way too many sunset photos online. But this one was impossible to ignore. Alec must have thought so, too, because he plopped down right where we were in the grass, gently tugging me down with him.

I sat with my knees up, my arms wrapped around them. Out there, in the middle of nowhere, you could hear everything: crickets singing and owls hooting and, in the distance, something I couldn't quite figure out.

"What is that?" I asked Alec.

"What?" He cocked his ear to the side, listening.

I waited. And then—

"That!"

"Oh, those are frogs."

"There are frogs here?"

"Yeah, over by the creek."

"They're so loud," I said, smiling. I loved it there.

And maybe it was the sunset, or the frogs' songs, or just being in Pearl Creek with Alec and his extremely cool family, but I wanted to be close to him. I scooted over without leaving an inch of space between us. Then I leaned my head on his shoulder, closing my eyes to take it all in.

Alec and I weren't super affectionate friends. He'd give me a half hug or a shoulder nudge, but we were mostly about high fives and fist bumps. He didn't shrug away from me. He put his arm around me, pulling me even closer.

We sat that way, watching the fading sky until the sizzling ball of orange dropped below the horizon.

"Look up," Alec said.

I did, and there were stars. So many more of them than back in Flores Hills. I stared at them until my eyes felt fuzzy.

It started to get cold, and I shivered. Alec rubbed my arm. "Should we go in?" he murmured. Still rubbing my arm.

I nodded and we stood. I turned to go back to the house, but Alec stopped me, his hand on my wrist.

"Marv?" He cleared his throat, stepping closer. "I really want to kiss you."

My eyebrows went up. Something had felt different

between us lately, especially here in Pearl Creek, but I didn't know what it was. I thought it was just us getting to know each other better. Was it more? Was it . . . this?

"So do it, Buckman," I said, sliding my hand around the back of his neck.

He did, and I kissed him back, and it was so nonsensical, me kissing Alec, but it also made all the sense in the world. His lips were soft and his mouth was warm, and it turned out Alec Buckman was quite the kisser. I shouldn't have been surprised, but I was, and that made me start laughing.

Alec pulled away, eyebrow raised. "Uh, Marv? Could you wait until *after* I stop kissing you to criticize me?"

"Oh my god, no," I said, bursting into a fresh peal of laughter. "I'm so sorry. It's not you. It's just . . ."

He had the hint of a laugh in his eyes, but he still looked a little skeptical, as if he wasn't quite sure I wasn't actually making fun of him.

I finally caught my breath and forced myself to focus. "I'm sorry. I was just thinking what a great kisser you are, and then, like, how dumb it was for me to be surprised. You're good at everything. Why not this?"

He squinted at me. "Are you just trying to make me feel better?"

"Not at all. You're perfect." Then I pulled him back down to me and kissed him first that time.

The air was different in Pearl Creek. *We* were different. There was something so deliciously calm and romantic about this place that when Alec touched my waist and pressed himself against me, I felt an intense need for him. A want that tore through me so rapidly and unexpectedly, it left me breathless.

We straightened our clothes and walked up to the main house, bumping elbows again until he grabbed my hand and kissed it.

His parents and Gertie and Frank were having cocktails in the living room as they listened to old jazz records. Gertie gave us a raised-eyebrow look, as if she knew exactly what we'd been up to, but they didn't say anything as we joined them, sitting on the floor cross-legged and close to each other, but without our knees touching. I sipped more lemonade while Frank told us about how his father turned him on to Mel Tormé records and how people no longer appreciated the kind of genius he brought to the table in the music world.

Gertie went to bed first, saying she had to get her rest for the festivities tomorrow. Alec's dad started yawning after that, then his mother; they walked down the hall to their room a few minutes later. Then it was just me, Alec, and Frank, who talked about Louis Armstrong and Duke Ellington and Charlie Parker until he was silent, just enjoying the music. I looked over after a while and saw his eyes were closing. When he let out a loud snore, Alec lightly shook his arm and said, "Papa, you should go to bed. We'll put the records away."

His grandfather sleepily patted us both on our shoulders and stumbled down the hallway, saying he'd see us in the morning.

Alec and I didn't put the records away. At least not right then. We sat and listened to Coltrane, whose music I knew because he's one of my dad's favorites. I got the feeling things should be weirder with Alec and me. We'd exchanged a few private looks that evening when we thought no one was looking, but it wasn't weird. It felt... good thinking about kissing him. And I wanted to do more of it.

"Hey," he said, and when I turned to look at him, he was staring at my mouth. We kissed and, eventually, pulled away to catch our breath. "Marv, I don't want to stop doing this with you."

"Me either." I paused. My heart was going berserk, but I felt like I might burst if I didn't say it then. I felt it too strongly not to say something. "Should we . . . I mean, what if we tried being together?"

He gave me a goofy grin that made me instantly lightheaded. "You want to be with me? Like, be my girlfriend?"

"No," I said. "I want *you* to be my *boy*friend."

Alec shook his head, but he was laughing, and then he kissed me again. "Okay. Then it's decided. But you couldn't have brought this up earlier?"

I tilted my head to the side. "What do you mean?"

"Because now everyone's in bed and all I want to do is shout to the world that I'm Marva Sheridan's boyfriend."

We kissed and we kissed and we kissed.

That day, that night—the whole trip, in fact—had been so utterly perfect that I just expected the rest of it would be equally blissful. And everything was fine at first.

The next day was July Fourth, and we had a nice breakfast at home before heading out for the parade and fireworks. Alec and I exchanged glances that made me remember every part of the way his lips had felt on my mouth, and how his hand had felt cupped around my neck.

So I wish he hadn't put a stain on my memory when were on the way to downtown Pearl Creek. We were riding in the car with his grandparents, and Alec's parents were driving separately. Gertie looked back at me and smiled.

"Marva, I hope your family doesn't miss you too much today," she said. "It's nice that they let you celebrate with us."

"Oh, we don't really do much for the Fourth," I said. "We celebrate Juneteenth."

I didn't think Alec would know what it was, but when I saw Gertie and Frank were just as clueless, my heart sank a bit. I didn't expect every white person to know everything about Black history, but it was surprising how many didn't know anything besides stories involving Frederick Douglass, Martin Luther King Jr., and Rosa Parks. And even then, most of the stories are only half true. But at least Alec and his grandparents seemed curious about Juneteenth, which is more than most people.

I licked my lips before I began. "Well, it's June nineteenth. Enslaved people in Texas didn't find out until *two and a half years* after the Emancipation Proclamation that they were free. Not until 1865. So Black people celebrate it every year, and it's recognized by almost every state in the country, even though a lot of people don't know about it."

Gertie nodded. "How nice that your family celebrates it. What sorts of things do you do?"

"Everybody celebrates in their own way, like the Fourth of July. We go to a family friend's house and have a cookout. Red foods are a big part of the tradition. We always have red velvet cake, hot links, a red drink, like strawberry soda, and watermelon."

But that description is nothing like actually being there celebrating. This year everyone seemed especially happy to be together. It felt like a mini family reunion, even though the Baxters hosted several other families and I didn't know everyone all that well. Juneteenth signs decorated the front lawn, which Mrs. Baxter assured me would be replaced with political signs when the time came. There was music and dancing, and games for the little kids. I mostly hung out with my parents and observed everyone paying tribute to their ancestors the best way we knew how: celebrating Black culture and the community that kept it thriving.

"That sounds lovely," Gertie said. "It's important to keep traditions alive."

Alec wrinkled his nose. "I don't get it. Why not just celebrate the Fourth?"

"What? I just told you the reason we recognize Juneteenth."

"Yeah, but what's the point of two separate holidays? I don't care if you're black, white, blue, or green—we're all American, right? Seems like we should be celebrating *together*, not encouraging divisiveness."

In the front seat, Gertie and Frank glanced at each other, but neither of them spoke.

"That's kind of an ignorant thing to say," I mumbled, my heart stuttering with each word. Alec and I hadn't really argued as friends, but now he was my boyfriend. For only about the past twelve hours, but still. Should we be disagreeing like this already?

He bristled, his hand stiffening in mine. "I'm not ignorant."

"No, you're not, so you shouldn't say things like that. First of all, blue and green people don't exist, so that's a ridiculous statement. And a hundred and fifty years of freedom doesn't erase four *centuries* of bondage and oppression, Alec. Black people weren't even free when the Declaration of Independence was adopted. Some people celebrate both, but it makes more sense to me to celebrate Juneteenth instead. I'm not going to feel bad about that."

"Well said," Frank murmured, the first time he'd spoken since we set off in the car.

Alec was quiet for a moment, then he said, "I guess I never thought about it like that."

"It would do you some good to listen instead of getting defensive next time," Gertie said in a soft voice, looking at him from the corner of her eye.

He swallowed and nodded. "That's fair, Nana." Then he leaned in. Whispered in my ear, "Sorry, Marv. I'm a dumbass."

I squeezed his hand to let him know I accepted his apology. With anyone else, that would have been a red flag. But I knew Alec and what he believed in.

Nobody was truly perfect.

DUKE

I'M NEVER GONNA GET TO THE FRONT OF THIS line. It's wrapped around the church, and nobody seems to be going in or out. Marva is still talking to her dude, so I take a few minutes to catch up on my texts.

There's another one from Anthony, saying the calculus test kicked his ass. Svetlana charged into the band's group chat, demanding to know if I'm sick and if I'll be at tonight's show. Benicio slides in with the occasional emoji, and Kendall says nothing at all. I wonder if the band has figured out she's not talking to me. Guess I'll find out tonight.

I scroll down through my messages until I get to her name. A little over two weeks ago is the last time we texted. I was apologizing, hoping it got through to her since the one I'd tried at the bonfire earlier that night didn't go over so well; she'd turned around as soon I walked up, icing me out with her girls. She texted back the next morning saying, *Please leave me alone, Duke.*

My thumbs hover over my phone for a few moments, as I try to think of the thing that will piss her off the least. I go with:

Thanks again for getting us the show tonight

Gonna be dope

And I promise myself this is the last time I'll bother her. But every time I think about Kendall, I flash back to that hurt look on her face in the kitchen. Like she'd been slapped. And it was my fault. For not being man enough to be honest with her about how nervous I felt around her, now that we know each other in real life.

I wait for some type of response. Anything. I'd even take that annoying little bubble that shows she's typing and then disappears when she changes her mind about talking to me. I get nothing.

I take a deep breath and close my eyes. I'm starting to wish I'd stayed in bed this morning.

When I open them a minute later, I realize Marva's been gone kind of a long time. That can't be a good conversation. I look around the church grounds to see if I can find her. She's standing next to a tree with her arms slack at her sides, staring at the sky. Def not a good conversation.

I'd go check on her, but I get the feeling she'd be pissed at me for losing my place in line just to make sure she was all right.

All kinds of people are standing in line, shifting impatiently and checking their phones and staring off into space like they wish they could teleport themselves someplace else. Most people are older than us, but there are a few kids our age. I hope Marva notices. We're not the only ones who care.

"Is this thing even moving?" I mutter under my breath.

"Slowly, but yes," the man in front of me says, turning around as if I was talking to him. He's older, with dark brown skin and gnarled fingers tightly gripping a cane. "Feel like I been standing in line all day."

"You've been here that long?" My stomach drops as I stare at all the people ahead of us.

"Nah, got up early and went to the place I've been voting for the last thirty years, and can you believe it was closed up? Nobody there, no sign. Spent half the day making all these phone calls to find out the city closed it and I had to come here instead." He shakes his head. "Flores Hills Senior Center chartered a bus to the original place, but once that was closed up, we were on our own to get here. It's all the way across town, by the hospital. I bet about half the people couldn't make it down here. Don't know what I would've done if I hadn't had the time and money to catch a city bus."

"All these people are with you?"

"Not all, but a good lot."

"That's ridiculous," says a voice next to me. I look over to see Marva, who managed to sneak over when I wasn't looking. "Honestly, it's like they're trying to do everything they can to keep people from voting!"

A smile peeks out from the man's wrinkled face, but it's not a happy one. "That ain't nothing new. Been happening since they were counting us as three-fifths of a human."

"That's the truth," Marva says, folding her arms.

The woman in front of him turns around to ask him something, and I look at Marva. "How'd it go with, uh, Alec?" I ask.

She doesn't look at me. "I don't think I'm going to have a boyfriend tomorrow."

"That bad? Shit. I'm real sorry, Marva."

"It's not your fault," she says.

"If I hadn't answered your—"

"No, I mean, I think maybe Alec and I aren't supposed to be together. Things have been... *off* for a while. It feels..." She shakes her head, trailing off.

"What?"

Marva looks at me now. "It feels like he's trying to pick a fight with me, and I don't get it. Why spend so much time fighting for things and then disappear when your voice is actually needed?"

"Wait, why is he picking a fight with *you*? Isn't he the one who went back on his word?"

"Exactly." She sighs. "He's totally in the wrong here, but he thinks it looks bad if he's mad at me, so he tries to get *me* to be mad at *him*."

I frown. "I don't get it."

She takes a deep breath. "I *don't* think all the time about how I'm a Black girl dating a white guy. But I see how people at Salinas Prep treat us. Part of it is because Alec is a big deal there. Everyone loves him. And he knows it, and never wants to look like the bad guy. So even if we're annoyed with each other, he'll never let on in front of anyone else."

"That sounds... like a lot of work."

"Right? But, also, I give him some street cred."

"Street cred?"

"There are eight Black kids in the whole school. Alec knows a lot of people think he's, like, *down* for dating me. And they make sure we know how cool they are with it, too. They always want me to know that I'm not different from them at all." She rolls her eyes.

"Oh," I say, nodding. "The whole 'you're not really Black' thing?"

"Yeah, exactly. You get that, too?"

"People don't expect to see a Black guy in an indie band. Every time I mention music, people think I'm a rapper. And Anthony *does* rap sometimes, but he's white. He's pretty dope, but I can't spit bars to save my life."

Marva groans. "What is *wrong* with people? We're either too Black or not Black enough."

"Try being only half Black," I say with a short laugh. "I'm never what people think I should be."

She nods, but she looks sad. I feel bad for her. This day can't be going like she thought it would.

"Hey," I say, "have you thought more about putting up a post on Eartha Kitty's account? We could do it now, while we're killing time? I have this app that makes pretty decent graphics. Could have one up in ten minutes."

She licks her lips, thinking. I haven't stopped noticing

her mouth, but I feel bad thinking about her like that. She *does* still have a boyfriend, no matter how shitty things are going. And it's never cool to go after another guy's girl. No matter how cute and smart and... *something* she is.

Her voice is almost a whisper when she says, "What if people find out I'm the one behind the account?"

"So what?"

"I'm... not the kind of person who would have an account like that." She sees the frown on my face and adds, "Who did you think was running that before you knew it was me?"

"I guess I never thought about it?"

"But you were surprised when you found out it was me, right?"

"I mean, I don't really know you—"

"Duke."

I shrug, shoving my hands in my pockets. "I don't know. Yeah, I mean, I guess I would've expected it to be someone less serious."

"See?"

"Serious isn't a bad thing." Julian was serious. He also liked dad jokes, and Monty Python, and playing harmless pranks he blamed on me. "It doesn't mean you can't have fun, too."

"But people won't take *me* seriously if they know that's my account."

"Come on. You want your cat back or not?"

She folds her arms in front of her chest.

"You don't have to put your address on there. Just give the general area. Open your DMs. Maybe make an email address for anyone who might be able to help."

"She already has an email address," Marva mutters.

"Perfect. I'll make a graphic now."

I grab my phone, expecting her to stop me, but she doesn't say a word. Just watches as I pull up the app and get to work.

The line does move, even if it's the slowest line in the history of lines. Marva talks to the old man ahead of us some more as I make the graphic. I'm half listening as they talk. He says his name is Clive, and he tells us he's been voting since the late fifties.

"You had to be twenty-one then, and people weren't happy 'bout that, since you could be drafted at eighteen. Didn't change it until 1970," he says, shaking his head. "Makes no sense how they were willing to send boys off to war but wouldn't let 'em vote for the commander in chief."

"Still, those were the good old days when *everyone* used paper ballots," says the woman in front of him. She's older, too. A white woman with a wig of gray curls piled on top of her head. "Didn't have to worry about all this technology and tampering with machines."

"I don't care what they use," says a woman behind us who overhears. "I just want to get in there soon. I have to get back to work before my lunch break is over, or my boss is going to write me up."

"I know the feeling," a softspoken man's voice says right after her. "I've gotta pick up my kid."

"There has to be a better way," Marva pipes up. "How can we vote in the people who want to make it easier for us to vote if we can't *get in* to vote in the first place?"

"That's the whole point," the wig lady says.

I tune them out for a couple of minutes to look over the graphic. It's simple. Black letters on a white background with a headline that says:

EARTHA KITTY IS MISSING

Clear and right to the point. As many followers as she has, people are gonna start looking for Eartha Kitty as soon as they see this.

I show it to Marva. She approves it, even though I can see the anxiety in her eyes.

"You're doing the right thing," I say.

She posts it, closes out of the app, and tucks her phone in her pocket, shuddering. “I hope so.”

I update the band in our group chat that I’ve been caught up trying to vote, but I’ll be at Anthony’s later to load my gear into the van and head over to the gig. We go on at eight, but we need to be at the Fractal early to warm up. I put the conversation on mute and pocket my phone when they start asking too many questions: Where the hell am I? Is it true some strange girl gave my sister and me a ride to FHH this morning? Because that’s what Ida said?

Marva and I pass some of the time by playing rock, paper, scissors. Marva is good, and she calls it “roshambo,” which makes me laugh.

“Where’d you learn that fancy name?”

“Well,” she says, pausing to crush me yet again with a rock over my scissors, “there’s a story that says it goes back to the comte de Rochambeau, this French guy who commanded the US troops that fought the British. But other people say that’s a myth. I don’t know. I just like the way it sounds.”

“I’ve never met anyone like you, Marva Sheridan,” I say, laughing as we start up another round.

Finally, we make it into the church for the second time today.

"About damn time," Clive says, shuffling in ahead of us.

Marva holds my place in line while I walk over to ask a poll worker about same-day registration. She hooks me up with a form and I fill it out at the edge of the table. She looks it over, nods, and initials a couple of boxes at the top.

"Hand this to the people manning the ballots when you make it up there," she says, handing it back to me. "And make sure you have your ID along with proof of residency if your ID's address isn't current."

"I've got everything," I say, patting my wallet. "I'm an old pro at this by now."

She gives me a tired smile. I get back in line next to Marva, who gives me the same type of smile when I show her the form.

Ten minutes later, there are finally, *finally* only two people ahead of us before we get to the table: Clive and the woman in the wig. And there's some sort of commotion. The woman is getting loud and the poll workers are trying to calm her down, but she's not having it. The people in the voting booths start turning around, and the poll workers are standing now, huddled around one another as they all try to calm down the woman. A rumble starts in the line behind us.

"What's going on?" Clive calls out.

"They ran out of ballots!" the woman ahead of him shouts.

Marva's mouth drops open. "What?"

"You gotta be kidding me," I mumble.

"This place is a goddamn joke," says someone a few people back in line.

"Don't you take the Lord's name in vain," someone else chastises them. "We're in His house."

"Um, everyone?" It's the red-haired woman with the braid from earlier this morning. She's standing on her tiptoes, trying to get everyone's attention by cupping her hands around her mouth. I only hear her because of how close we are.

It's clear she's not going to get anyone to shut up, so I stick my fingers in my mouth and blow out a long, steady whistle like Julian taught me. A long time ago, but I never forgot it.

Marva stares at me. "I've been trying to figure out how to do that for years."

"It's not that hard," I mumble. "I'll teach you."

The woman at the table throws a grateful look my way,

then starts talking before she loses the silence. "Everyone, I'm so sorry, but we've run out of ballots. We've had quite a few voters we didn't anticipate due to another location's closure."

"So what are we supposed to do now?" Marva asks. "We've been waiting here forever."

"This is some *bullshit*," Clive says, shaking his head. "You trying to tell me I spent all morning figuring out where I had to go, fought my way onto a packed bus to get here, waited in line for damn near two hours, and you *ran out of ballots*?" He shakes his cane at the woman. "This ain't right. You *know* it ain't right."

"Sir, I'm sorry," the woman says. "Everyone, *we're sorry*. We didn't plan for the unusually high turnout. We *will* get more ballots, but we'll have to wait for the city clerk to deliver them."

"How long's that going to take?" Marva asks.

The woman sighs. "I'm honestly not sure. A couple of hours? Maybe longer?"

The crowd erupts into one huge, angry roar.

Beside me, Marva's whole body sags.

MARVA

MY HOPE IS FADING.

It's as if I can physically feel it draining from my body, limb by limb. Like I could just sit down on the floor right now and give up, because I can't believe, after all we've been through, that they've run out of ballots.

As I look around, I see a whole variety of reactions: anger, fatigue, defeat. Not one happy face in the crowd. Hopelessness fills the air.

I don't even bother saying anything to Duke before I turn on my heel, cut through the line of people behind us, and storm out of the church doors.

A few seconds later, I hear Duke's now-familiar footsteps behind me. "Hey," he says. "Hey, Marva. Hey!"

I stop but don't turn around.

"It's gonna be okay," he says.

And then, suddenly, my hopelessness turns to rage. White-hot anger at this whole backward system that takes full days out of people's lives just so they can have some say in how their country is run. Clive said it best earlier: *This is some bullshit.*

"No, it's not, Duke. It's *not* okay! What the hell are we supposed to do?" I take the biggest breath possible. Let it out. It doesn't help. I turn around.

Duke looks as drained as I feel, but his eyes are soft as they land on me. Like in this moment he's more concerned about how upset I am than the cause of my anger.

"We'll come back in a couple of hours and they'll have the ballots and everything will be fine. I promise."

I don't say anything. I appreciate how he's trying to make me feel better, but it doesn't help anything. Not for me or that entire crowd of people we just left behind. I turn around and start walking again, away from the church.

He takes a couple of long strides to catch up with me, and before I can get far at all, I feel his hand on my shoulder. "It's not over, Marva."

"Isn't it, though?" Keeping such high standards for myself and the people around me means disappointment hits hard when something doesn't go my way. But this... this is next-level disappointment. With Selma going missing and Alec pissed at me, I needed *one* thing to go right this afternoon. I wish I could scrounge up that feeling of pride and accomplishment from this morning, after I cast the first vote here. But... I don't know. It almost feels like an empty vote if not everyone gets the chance to cast theirs, too.

I face Duke again. You'd never know all the hoops we've jumped through so far today by looking at him. He's so calm. He looks tired from all the running around we've done, and definitely frustrated—but with an underlying chill. And I don't understand how he can just keep his cool like this. "You see how many people are *here* who still haven't been able to vote—imagine this all over town. All over the state. All over the country! What Clive said is true. This isn't right."

"I know," Duke says. "It's not. But we're not giving up. We're just taking a break. Because there's nothing else we can do now."

He's right. I don't like that he is, but he's right.

"It's just... I spent so much time over the last two years

working up to this point, and so did a lot of other people. And it just doesn't seem fair that all that work means nothing when the actual day is here." I swallow hard. "Duke, what if things don't go our way? What if this country keeps moving backward?"

"I know," he says, inhaling. "I know. But this isn't all up to *you* to fix. You've done more today than most people will do in their lifetimes. Just to make sure some knucklehead like me can vote."

That makes me smile. Just a little bit. "Knucklehead?"

He shrugs. "It's what Ida calls me. I don't fight it anymore." He pauses, then his eyes light up. The brightest they've been since we were eating fried bologna sandwiches. "Listen, I think we need a break. From all of this."

"What do you mean?"

"I mean, can I take you somewhere? It's not too far, and I'll drive. I'm a good driver. I promise not to crash the Volvo. And you could probably use a break from driving."

I start to say no way am I letting him behind the wheel of my car, when I realize how nice that was. He's been appreciative of me driving him around today, but offering to take the reins is exactly what I need right now. It's thoughtful. Kind.

I give him a look. “Are you just offering because my driving scares you?”

He grins. “Nah, I’m accustomed to fearing for my life by now.”

“Very funny.” But that warrants a real smile. I’m getting used to his teasing. I don’t mind it.

“What do you say? We have to kill some more time anyway.”

I toss my keys at him before I overthink it. “Fine. But if you put so much as a scratch on the Volvo, I’m sending Terrell after your ass.”

“Please. Terrell and I are homies,” he says, catching them in his big, cupped hands. “Come on. Let’s get out of here.”

I don’t like surprises.

And not knowing where I’m going usually makes me nervous. But after the stress of today, I can’t let myself get too worked up about it. I keep thinking of Selma out there all alone, and all the people we talked to in line who went through even more than we did just to vote today. What if they just go home, frustrated at getting turned away after all they’ve done to get there? What if Selma *never* comes home? I don't even have the heart to see how the latest post went over on her account.

Duke doesn't say much as we drive. He asks if he can turn on the radio, and when I say yes, he changes it to a rock station. I don't know the song, but he drums against my steering wheel almost the whole drive. It should annoy me, but I don't know. It's kind of cute how he's so into music.

Once we're on the freeway, about twenty minutes outside of Flores Hills, I think I know where we're headed.

"The beach?" I ask once I see official signs for it.

"Yeah. Is that cool?"

"It's cool." I'm not really a beach person, but as Mom would say, I'm not *not* a beach person. It's close enough to go, but never my first choice.

"We always go to the beach when we cut, so I figured why not today?" Duke says. "Doesn't feel right otherwise."

"How often do you skip school?" I ask, incredulous that he has a whole routine planned around it.

"More than you, I'm guessing." He grins. "But not too much. It still has to feel like I'm getting away with something, you know?"

I think I know what he means. Because even though I haven't set foot in school all day, it feels like I'm getting away with something, too. I don't really take breaks from problems until they're solved, and I've got plenty of them today. But getting away from them, even for just a little bit, feels like the best thing I can do for myself right now.

I can't help but smile back at him. The more time I spend with Duke Crenshaw, the more he's actually starting to make sense to me.

DUKE

THANKSGIVING IS THREE WEEKS AWAY, BUT IT'S hot as hell out today. The heat drops the closer you are to the shore, so by the time we park, walk down to the beach, and get on the sand, I got my arms out at my sides, taking in the breeze.

"Those things are like propellers," Marva mutters, ducking. Even though she's not walking close enough for me to touch her.

"Try again," I say, closing my eyes against the breeze.

"What?"

And I just get this feeling that she's giving me a weird look, even though I can't see her.

"You think I haven't heard that one before? With arms this long?"

When I open my eyes, she's frowning. "I didn't mean anything by it."

"I'm just saying, every name in the book for someone my size? I've heard it. Big Duke. Tiny. Giraffe. Insert just about any ballplayer's name."

She folds her hands into the pocket of her hoodie. "Okay. Sorry for objectifying you, Big Duke."

I throw my hands up, staring at her in disbelief. "It's a thing. Do you know how many times I have to hear *How's the weather up there?*" I make a visor with my hand and peer up at the sky like people stare at me sometimes. "It's annoying."

She knocks her elbow against mine—or tries to, but I'm so tall that her arm hits my hip instead and she jumps back a little, surprised. Maybe embarrassed, too, by the way she immediately looks away. Which is all kinda perfect for this conversation.

"Want to go to the pier?" I ask, following her gaze.

It's a small pier, because the beach is small. But there

are a couple of gift shops and stands selling ice cream and hot dogs.

"No," she says, shaking her head. Then she looks at me. "When was the last time you were at the beach?"

We move down the sand to the water. The closer we get, the better I feel. After Julian died, my therapist asked about places that I feel calm. The beach was number one. There's something about the ocean. Maybe because it's one of the only things that makes me feel truly small. It reminds me that there are things bigger than me, the six-foot-three kid with the dead brother.

"A couple weeks ago," I say. "Bonfire."

That was the last time Kendall bothered to look at me. I deserved it, but I hate the guilt that twists up in my stomach every time I think about what I said to her. And how my dumb mouth wrecked the friendship we'd built over the last couple of years. If it had been any other girl, I probably wouldn't still be thinking of this. But Kendall . . . she's not just our manager.

I guess I met her at exactly the right time. Food didn't taste the same. Stuff I used to love, like Ma's key lime pie and Dad's famous lasagna, could've been dirt, the way I felt. I started being able to tune people out real good, their voices turning to nonsense as they stood right in front of me. People got tired of having one-sided conversations, so they stopped talking to me little by little until everyone eventually just left me alone.

Ida and I went to talk to a therapist once a week. I liked Dr. Darby, but I could only go so deep with her. It wasn't easy to sit across from a strange woman and pour my guts out about my dead brother.

I was messing around online one night when I found the forum. I was thinking about Julian, which I guess made me type in:

What to do when your brother dies

I didn't expect anything helpful to pop up. The internet can be a trash pit, which I'm reminded of every time a Black person died in some public way. Even the articles about Julian, who had a good rep in the community, were filled with nasty reader comments at the bottom. People said things like he must have been a thug, and wasn't it ironic that the guy who was so concerned about gun violence got killed by Black-on-Black crime, and more bullshit that made me feel like my eyes would bleed.

But page after page came up on my search. Some of them were articles posted on medical and psychology websites. General advice about how to handle grief. I kept scrolling until I got to the forums, where it was real people like me posting about what it felt like.

I couldn't relate to the first forum I found. Most of it was about losing spouses or parents. And when it was about siblings, they were grieving over a brother or sister who'd died when they were in their forties or fifties. Most of them had had almost a lifetime with the person; I only had Julian for sixteen years.

But then I came across a link to a forum for teens, and the more I read, the more I started nodding, agreeing with everything they said. Like how it was hard to concentrate at school now, and how people did fucked-up things like compare your sibling's death to their grandparents who had passed away from natural causes in their eighties. I read as much as I could until my eyes started drooping. Then, for the first time since Julian died, I slept through the night.

I started going on the forums every night before bed. Not just because it seemed like some sort of sleeping pill, but also because it made me feel better. When things started getting too cluttered in my head, it cleared my mind to scroll through the forum and read about people who were feeling the exact same way for the exact same reason.

I talked to everybody at first, then realized I was replying more to only certain people. Especially one person. She called herself Mz K, and her avatar was a dumb-looking purple unicorn, which made me laugh every time I logged on. Once, we were posting so much back and forth in the same forum that she finally DMed me.

Figured we should take this offline to spare everyone

I dug her dry sense of humor and how she knew the director, screenwriter, and lead actors from every single rom-com made from the 1960s on, and how she was just so *real*. Her brother had also been shot, but he'd been in a gang and they knew who killed him. Sometimes I felt guilty for getting as angry as I did—*I* was still alive—but Mz K never did. She'd start out messages some days by saying *I woke up so fucking pissed today*. And I got it. Every time.

We started texting after about a month of talking online, and that's when she told me her name. Kendall Ford from Flores Hills. I looked her up. Not a lot came up except little profile pictures I could barely see, since her social media was private. So I was glad when she sent me a picture of herself a couple of days after we'd been texting.

I looked at it off and on for hours. She was pretty: light brown skin and black hair with bangs that swooped across her forehead, and braces she said were going to be taken off in three weeks. I hadn't ever been on a date. Not even a school dance, because I got shy around girls and I'd always felt too stupid to ask Julian for advice.

I spent way too long taking a selfie good enough to send her, then fired it off before I could change my mind. She wrote back right away: *You're cute*

I couldn't stop smiling as I typed back: *So are you*

We texted constantly, sometimes until one or two in the morning. I felt like there was nothing I couldn't tell her.

So when Ma and Dad said we were moving a couple of hours away, to Flores Hills, I freaked out. I'd be going to the same high school as Kendall. We were in the same grade. This girl, who knew everything about me, was going to be so close. Close enough to see all the time.

I guess I messed up from the start with Kendall because I didn't tell her I was moving. I don't know why. We'd never even had an argument, but I felt weird about moving into her space. What if she didn't want me there? I was just this strange guy who lived in her phone.

I saw her almost as soon as I got to FHH that first day, which was weird. It's a big school. But there she was, at her locker, laughing with her girls. My heart started beating fast as soon as I recognized her. Her braces were off and she had pretty teeth, too. I told myself to go over and say something, but instead I went to find my locker before the first bell.

She was in my English class. I was already sitting at the back of the room when she walked in. I watched her find a seat near the window, up front. She didn't glance back once, and I should have said something, but I didn't.

I cringed my way through the first few names of roll call and tried to make myself as small as possible when Mr. Johnson called out, "Duke Crenshaw?"

Her head was down as she doodled in her journal, but as soon as I said "Here," my name must have worked itself up into her brain. Even though it was out of place here. Even though what were the chances of there being a Duke Crenshaw in her English class at Flores Hills that she actually knew?

She set her pencil down and her head came up. She turned slowly in her seat to look in the direction of my voice. We locked eyes. Her lips parted and she stared at me for several seconds, until Mr. Johnson got to the *F* part of the alphabet and called her name.

Kendall kept sneaking looks at me, and I kept looking back at her. Finally, she mouthed, "Is it you?"

I nodded. She turned around to face the front. I saw her hand shaking when she picked up her pencil again.

She packed up her things right away after class and headed out of the room without even looking my way. Great. I'd already fucked up and it was only my first day here. I wondered when I would see her again, but as I stepped out of the classroom, someone said, "Hey." I looked over to my left and she was there.

Looking confused and hurt, but there. Her eyebrows went up and down as she said, "Duke, what are you doing here?"

"We moved."

She pursed her lips at me. "Obviously."

"My parents wanted us to come down here for a fresh start." I didn't mention that they'd been fighting more than ever, and I was pretty sure Dad had been sleeping in the guest room ever since we got to the new house.

"But you knew you were moving to Flores Hills and didn't say anything?" She shook her head. "Why didn't you tell me?"

It was weird being next to her in the flesh. As much as we talked, it was never over the phone. Just DMs and then texts. Every time she'd suggested we actually talk so we could hear each other's voices, I said I hated being on the phone. I didn't tell her it made me nervous. That I worried she wouldn't like me if she got to know all of me.

"I don't know. Because I'm a jerk? I'm sorry, Kendall."

She sighed and blinked at me. She smelled good. Like flowers. And her hair was so shiny up close. I was trying not to stare at her too hard, but it's like I couldn't believe she was an actual living, breathing person. Over the next few days, I caught her looking at me the same way.

She forgave me. And we slowly became friends in real life, too. Texting still, but now we ate lunch together and stopped by each other's locker, and sometimes I gave her a ride home from school because I already had my license.

Then, once we started up Drugstore Sorrow, Kendall started coming to practices every once in a while. Even when we were *real* bad, she supported us. I think Svetlana was the one who suggested Kendall be our manager, and we were all on board.

But that's when I started to feel a little funny about things. We weren't dating, but we hung out so much that I think some people wondered if we were. Even in the band. And now we'd be together even more than we already were.

I knew Kendall *liked* me, but I couldn't go there. I guess it would look to some people like I was leading her on, but I needed her to be my friend. If we went further, I would mess things up. I knew it. And I didn't want to lose her, too.

Not after I'd already lost someone so important to me.

But now it looks like I've lost her anyway. She still hasn't texted back—not to me or the group chat.

I glance down the beach at the spot where we all were a couple weeks ago, then look at Marva. "You go to bonfires?"

She shrugs. "No . . . not really."

"What do you do for fun?"

She pauses. "I'm with Alec a lot. And our friends. I volunteer. I've been doing a lot of campaigning the past two years. I study."

I laugh. "Studying isn't something you do for fun."

"Speak for yourself." Marva chews her lip, trying not to smile.

I take off my socks and shoes, chuck them behind me, and walk into the rolling tide, forgetting too late that I didn't hike up the bottom of my jeans. Oh, well. Water dries.

"Feels good," I say, turning to look at Marva.

"I'll take your word for it." She stands stick-straight back by my shoes.

I turn to the ocean and stand there. Just listening. Taking in everything. The seagulls cawing as they swoop down and try to eat up everybody's food. Little kids with plastic beach toys building sandcastles and tunnels. Tourists soaking up every ounce of sun they can get.

"What time do you think we should head back?" Marva's standing a few feet behind me now, just at the water's edge.

"Are you for real? We just got here. School's out, so you don't need to be there. Can't you just relax?" I thought coming here would be good for her. Maybe help her chill a little. I'm starting to wonder if that's actually possible.

"Ugh," she says under her breath.

"What?"

"It's just . . . Do you really live like this?"

"Like what?"

"Like, everything's just sooo chill allllll the time," she says in this lazy stoner voice that makes me laugh.

"Is that what you really think?"

"How could I not? Honestly, it's like nothing ever bothers you."

"Lots of stuff bothers me," I say. "But maybe not as much as it bothers you."

"Tell me something I don't know," she mutters.

"Or maybe I just deal with it differently. Like, it sounds corny as hell, but my happy place is the beach. I feel better here than just about anywhere else, you know?"

She's quiet.

"Do you have somewhere that makes you feel like that?"

"I . . . I don't know," she says, looking down at the sand.

"Well, just try to chill. Enjoy where you are. Stop worrying for a second that everything isn't going to work out, and put your damn toes in the water."

She opens her mouth like she's about to object, but then closes it. And bends down to untie her combat boots. Marva looks at me for a moment, then throws her boots and socks back by mine and walks up to stand next to me.

She lets out what sounds like something close to a happy sigh.

"Worth it?" I ask, glancing over.

"Shut up and let me enjoy where I am," she replies, her face tipped toward the sky.

MARVA

I WOULD NEVER ADMIT THIS OUT LOUD, BUT DEEP down, a part of me does feel good that I skipped school today.

It feels like maybe, if one thing gets off track, my whole life won't fall apart. Of course Selma is still missing, and I feel sick wondering if those ballots will ever show up at the church, and Alec and I are not in a good place.

But it is kind of impossible to resist the sun, the waves, the salty air. Duke is right. When I just close my eyes and breathe, I feel a little calmer. My head feels clearer.

"When was the last time *you* were at the beach?" Duke asks, squinting at me to keep the sun out of his eyes.

I think. And think. And keep thinking. "I actually can't remember. Maybe a year or two ago?"

The last time was probably when my aunt and uncle came to visit.

"*Years?*" Duke's mouth hangs open in absolute horror. "You gotta be kidding me. It's only a half hour away. Do you swim?"

"I can," I say. "My parents had me in swimming lessons as a baby. Said it wasn't right to live this near the ocean and not know how to swim. I guess I loved it as a kid, but it's not my favorite or anything. I'm better on dry land."

"Well, I've lived near enough the water my whole life, too, but I can't swim for shit."

"Really?"

"Yeah, I took lessons, but they never stuck."

"Doesn't the ocean scare you? It's so big."

"That's why I love it," Duke says. "I mean, we only have a tiny idea of what the hell is living down there. That's pretty badass."

I shake my head. "No, thank you."

Then I close my eyes and breathe in, because even if

the ocean scares me, I like being on this side of it. Shoes at the ready, sand beneath my toes. I flex them under the ripples of water, inhaling again, and—

Suddenly I'm cold. And wet.

"Oh my god!" I shriek, eyes flying open. "What are you doing?"

Water is *dripping* down my face. Trailing down my neck and into my bra, and Duke is doubled over laughing at his successful splash attack.

I wipe my face with the backs of my hands, trying to remind myself it's just water. It will dry. But I don't like being wet when I'm not supposed to be. Sticking my toes in was more than I even wanted to do, really—

A second blast of water hits me and I scream again. "What is your *problem*?" I splutter. "Are you twelve?"

"Your face," Duke says, laughing so hard he can barely speak.

My murder face, I'm sure. Alec likes to comment on it when he does something that gets on my nerves. *If looks could kill* and all. Usually, getting splashed in the face with what feels like actual waves not once but twice would cause me to stomp away. And I think about it—leaving him stranded on the beach with no way to get home or back to his dead car in the church parking lot.

But—ugh. There's something about *his* face. It's the opposite of a murder face. It's joyous, like he's been transformed back into an actual twelve-year-old. And it's contagious. Because as salt water drips down my neck in rivulets, I start laughing. And before I know it, I'm bending down, scooping water into my hands, and splashing Duke—twice as hard as he splashed me.

Our water fight is short but intense as we dance around each other, ducking and dodging like we're in a beach ballet. Finally, when we're both out of breath from laughing and running, we stop, palms held up in a truce.

Duke moves his hands to the tops of his knees, chest heaving as he looks at me. "I thought you were going to kill me for a minute."

I smile sweetly at him. "I thought about it."

I'm glad I decided to stash my phone with my boots so it's not soaked. Mom is always saying how I need to leave my phone alone more, get out and enjoy the world and all it has to offer. But between my campaigning and maintaining Selma's social media account, I can't go too long without it. And I'm especially glad to have it on a day like today, so I can check the exit polls later. With our luck, who knows if I'll even be able to watch the results on TV?

"You feel better, right?" he says, finally catching his breath. "This place is magic."

I don't know about magic, but he's right. I feel better than when I came. Like maybe there's still some space for the hope I was filled with when I woke up this morning. And it's hard not to feel better when I look at him—his face is so open and happy right now, it's practically contagious.

"Yeah," I say with a small smile. "I feel better. Thanks."

We sit on the sand for a while, just watching the ocean and the people around it running, walking, sunbathing, surfing, playing Frisbee... Whatever I think about the beach, a lot of people seem to think it's magic, just like Duke. I look around and I don't see one frown. It's like time has stopped here and no one is worried about how the election is going to turn out or what that means for them and their friends and family and people around the world. Normally that would infuriate me, but I don't know. Maybe a little magic never hurt anyone.

But we have to leave eventually, and even I'm a little sad when the time comes.

"There might still be a long line," I finally say. "Probably better to head back to the church and make sure they don't run out of ballots *again*."

But I notice how slow our footsteps are on the way back to the car. And how wistful Duke looks before we've even made it all the way up the stairs to the parking lot.

"Thanks for letting me bring you here," he says, his eyes meeting mine briefly before he looks away. Shyly.

"Thanks for bringing me," I say as we near the Volvo. "I—"

At first I think I must be imagining this. Maybe I got too much sun. Because I recognize the car idling behind mine. The sleek gray Audi with tinted windows that I've sat in probably hundreds of times. But it couldn't be, right? It's probably just the same car as his. It has to be.

Except the passenger window rolls down and Alec is leaning over, looking at me from behind his Ray-Bans. "Hi."

I forgot that we have our phones linked so we can always track where the other one is. It was his idea, and I didn't think much about it, since we'd been together a year when he suggested it. I trusted him wholeheartedly. Plus, some of his friends had linked their accounts with their girlfriends' and boyfriends', so it didn't seem strange to me.

I never thought he'd use it because *I'd* violated *his* trust.

I only have to look at Duke for a couple of seconds

before he understands what's happening and says, "I'm gonna take a walk."

Alec barely waits for him to leave before he asks, "Was that your project for today?" He sneers it, really.

"What do you care?"

"Uh, maybe because you're my girlfriend?"

"But that's the thing, Alec!" I cry. "You haven't seemed to care much at all about me lately. It's what you want, all the time. Colleges, and now this voting thing..."

Alec's face takes on a hard edge as he slides his sunglasses on top of his head. "Jesus, don't you care about *anything* else?"

"And don't you care about *anything*? Alec, these issues affect me and a lot of the people I know and love. I don't have the luxury of just *not* voting, and you shouldn't take advantage of the fact that you do!"

He doesn't answer me, just stares straight ahead. He has no good argument for this, and I feel satisfied knowing I've technically won.

Except... something he said on the phone earlier keeps ringing in my ears. I'd shoved it away, not wanting to think too deeply about what it meant. But now...

I'm not changing my mind. And you're not going to change me, so maybe you should just give up now.

How could I have pushed that to the side when he was so clearly trying to tell me something? He wasn't just trying to get me to pick a fight with him. He—

"Are you trying to get me to break up with you?"

His jaw tenses. He doesn't deny it.

"Who the hell *are* you, Alec Buckman?"

"The same guy you've been dating for over two years."

"No, you're not," I say, pulse racing as our relationship flashes before my eyes at record speed. "You were so empathetic when I met you. You really cared about people and how they were treated and what we could do to help. That's so much of why I started liking you in the first place."

"I never said I was an activist," he mutters, leaning his head against the seat as if he's so utterly exhausted from talking to me.

"No, but you acted like one. That's even worse. Did you *ever* care about all the things you said you did? Or was it all an act? Something you were trying on for a while until you realized you actually *had* to care to fight for them?"

"I'm tired of being angry all the time, Marva!" he yells now, slamming his hand against the steering wheel. "You're always upset about something: guns, abortion, racism, immigration, healthcare...like, damn! I'm not saying those things aren't real problems, but it's depressing always thinking and talking and worrying about that stuff. Sometimes I need time off."

"Oh, well, I'm *so sorry* that *you* need a day off. Because you know what? Some of us don't get to take a day off, Alec! Some people don't even know if they're going to *see* another day, thanks to all the things you just named. And you're *tired*? Of being *angry*? Give me a break."

"Just because I'm white and have money doesn't mean I don't have problems," he says in a tight voice.

I close my eyes for a moment. Breathe in and out to regroup. Try to get this back on track. "I never said that. But your problems are different from other people's. You have the resources to help make their lives better, and it doesn't cost you much except actually putting other people's needs ahead of yours. Not all the time. Just sometimes. Like today."

Alec doesn't say anything for a long time. A family of five walks by us, laughing and shouting and lugging their beach gear. The littlest kid is in front of the family, hopping to try to catch seagulls that keep ducking in and out of the parking lot.

"I guess I'm not the guy you thought I was," he says, his gray eyes fixed on me.

And that's when I know. It's over.

This whole time he was telling me who he was, bit by bit, and I refused to see it. Or believe him.

I think of all the wonderful times we've had: getting all dressed up for school dances with corsages and boutonnieres; spending quiet nights in studying, stealing kisses between flash cards; taking long drives on Sunday afternoons with nothing but the sky and open land ahead of us . . . Alec Buckman has been such a big part of my life for the past two and a half years. I wouldn't have been nearly as happy at Salinas Prep without him by my side. He's the first guy I've ever loved, and I don't regret that.

But our problem isn't just about voting or colleges or our cultural differences. It's foundational. And I don't need someone in my life that I have to convince to do the right thing, over and over again.

"We need to break up," I say, and it's not as hard as I thought it would be.

He gives me an ugly look, and I don't get it. Isn't this what he wanted?

"Did you fuck that dude?"

"Fuck *you*, Alec," I say, my eyes narrowing. "You know I would never, ever do that to you. You don't have to be nasty."

He stares at me for a long time, his face cycling through half a dozen expressions before he finally settles on anger. The one emotion I thought he was tired of.

"Fine." He slips his Ray-Bans back on. "But don't try to come crawling back when this guy doesn't end up being the perfect person you want him to be. Who the hell can live up to your standards?"

"I'm not too worried," I say. "The bar was pretty low with you."

He scoffs, puts the car in drive, and peels out of the parking lot, tires squealing.

My shoulders sag. *I just broke up with Alec.* And I know, deep down, that it was the right thing to do, but my chest still hurts the same way it does on the last day of school or New Year's Eve or the night before my birthday. It's the end of a chapter in my life. And, yes, another one will eventually open where this one closed, but it's scary, taking away that piece of comfort. Of routine.

I hear footsteps; they are jogging and then they stop right behind me.

"You all right?"

"We just broke up," I say, my back still to him.

"Yeah, I figured. I'm, ah, sorry. I hope it wasn't my fault."

I turn around and Duke is so close I have to stretch my neck to look up at him. "It's not your fault. I think . . . he's not who I thought he was. And everything that happened today made me realize it."

"He doesn't deserve you," Duke says. His voice is soft, but not too soft. There's enough conviction behind it to make me know he's not just saying that to make me feel better.

We look at each other for a while. There is so much I want to say, and I think there's more *he* wants to say. But I'm too overwhelmed right now to make sense of the mess of emotions inside me.

So I say the only thing I know how to in this moment. "Thanks."

DUKE

"YO, HAVE YOU SEEN THE COMMENTS ON YOUR post? People are losing their shit about Eartha Kitty being missing," I say as we get in the car. I hold the phone out so she can see.

Marva is back to driving, and I don't object. I think it makes her feel better, and she looks so sad, I want to do whatever I can to make that happen. I know she said it wasn't my fault about her and her dude, but I can't help feeling like I had some small part in it.

"Really?" Marva puts the key into the ignition but doesn't start the car. She looks conflicted. Like she's not sure if she should even peek over at my phone. Finally, she does, and her eyebrows shoot to the ceiling. "Whoa."

I scroll through a few dozen comments. "Yeah, and they all want to help."

"Any leads?" she asks.

I shake my head. "Man, I don't even know. You'll need an assistant to get through all these. Is your phone dead yet?"

"I turned off the notifications."

"Damn, you really think of everything," I say, not even hiding how impressed I am. "I could help you go through them, if you want. Maybe we can send any leads to your dad?"

"I don't know if we have time for that." She glances at the dashboard clock. "I really don't want to miss out on the ballots."

But she's got her phone out, hesitantly pulling up the post as if her phone is going to explode once it's on her screen. She's silent as she looks through the comments. She smiles at a few of them, rolls her eyes, and nods every once in a while. Then she gets to one that stops her cold.

"Oh my god," she says in a low voice. A super-pissed-off voice. One I'm glad she's never used with me. Yet.

"What's up?"

"People know it's me."

I look over her shoulder at her screen, even though mine is right in front of me. She scrolls down to the last few comments, and I see them, too:

Marva Sheridan runs this account

OMG someone just told me this is Marva's cat!!!

Marva likes something besides studying? lol

I totally saw a pic of her with a cat once—it was TOTALLY Eartha Kitty holy shit

"Whoa. How'd they find out?" I ask. "I thought it was a big secret."

"It was. People know who Eartha Kitty is at Salinas Prep, but I've never, ever told anyone she belongs to me. The only person who knew was Alec." Her eyes narrow into the thinnest slits. "God, we broke up five minutes ago and this is the first thing he does? He doesn't even care that she's missing, he just wants to get back at me!"

"Guys do a lot of stupid shit when we're upset."

She turns her glare on me. "Don't you dare stick up for him!"

"I'm not. I'm just saying, this probably means he *does* care in some messed-up way."

"I don't give a shit if he cares," Marva snaps. "He's trying to humiliate me. Get the last word. And you know what? Fuck him."

"Yeah, fuck him," I echo.

Marva looks at me for a couple of seconds and I think she might be about to kill me. Then she busts out laughing. A loud, long laugh. I haven't heard her laugh like this since I met her, and it feels like when I hear a really good song for the first time and love it right away.

"He wants me to be embarrassed, so I'm going to do the opposite of what he wants. Do you mind taking a video of me?"

"Huh?"

"I'm going to post a live video on Eartha Kitty's account. And we're going to set up a *real* search party. If so many people want to help, we still have time to get them organized. Then we'll make sure you get back to the church to vote and you can still make it to your show. And hopefully someone will find my damn cat in the meantime."

Oh, yeah. My show. I'd almost forgotten about it. Which means this has been one hell of a day, because I never forget about a Drugstore Sorrow show. I'm usually nervous about it weeks before, but all that went right out the door when I linked up with Marva this morning.

"You sure you want to do this?" I ask as she checks herself out in the rearview mirror. I don't realize I'm checking her out, too, until she looks at me.

"Duke, yes! I've spent so much time worrying about what people think about me instead of letting them get to know *all* of me. What better time than now to set the record straight?"

"You got it, boss."

It's funny she thinks she needs to put on lip gloss and smooth down her braids and do all this other little stuff, because she looks perfect to me. Even when she was crying earlier, I thought how pretty she was. She looks pretty all the time, though—frowning and determined, or soft and sad. I'm here for all of it. For all of her.

She doesn't even want to get out of the car, so she sits with her back straight against the driver's side door and I hit RECORD when she tells me she's ready.

"Hi," she says. "My name is Marva Sheridan, and I'm the person who started this account. You haven't seen my face before on here, and you probably won't see it again anytime soon, but I want to thank everyone for all your nice messages about my cat today. She's been missing since this morning, and my family and I haven't been able to find her.

"So many of you mentioned in the comments that you wanted to help, so here I am—asking for your help. If you'd like to look for her, meet at the corner of French Street and Robinson Avenue as soon as you see this. I'm on my way there now. And if you start looking for her right away—well, you know her as Eartha Kitty. But her name is Selma. And I love her very much. Thank you."

She looks at me expectantly after I shut off the camera. "How was it?"

"Perfect."

"You're not just saying that?"

"It's too late now," I say. "That shit was live."

"Duke!"

I grin at her. "I'm kidding. It was dope. Anyone who sees that and doesn't want to help you find her isn't worth your time."

"You really think so?"

My hand brushes hers as I hand back her phone. I want to find a reason to touch her for longer, but I can't be that dude. The one who tries to get with a girl ten seconds after she breaks up with her boyfriend.

And I still feel weird about how things are going between Kendall and me. Or not going. We weren't ever together, but I need to fix what I did before I even think about another girl. Julian would say I need to man up and take responsibility for my actions.

Probably the weirdest part about this day is how I feel like I've actually done something to help someone. I can't remember the last time I felt useful. Like, yeah, I play in Drugstore Sorrow and sometimes I help out my sister when she needs it, but that's just part of my everyday life. This . . . this is different.

It feels almost like when I met Kendall on the forum and she made me realize that not talking about my problems wasn't doing me any good. That I could process things however I wanted, but I needed to process them. Somehow. I had to make a change.

I wish Kendall could've talked to my dad. Everyone in my family was having a hard time with Julian's death, but I'm pretty sure it hit him the hardest.

Then, like he knows I'm thinking about him, a text comes through. The first sign of communication since the angry messages I pulled up at Marva's house.

You ignoring me now?

Boy you may be 18 but you not grown

Call me

ABOUT DAD.

MY DAD WAS NEVER LIKE A TV FATHER OR ANYTHING.

Scratch that. He's kinda like one of those super-old-school dads on black-and-white shows who'd come home from work, kick up their feet, and read the newspaper until dinner was ready. He helped out around the house when we all lived together—it's not like he made Ma do everything. But he's a quiet dude and pretty hands-off when it comes to talking about problems.

He's not really down with cracking dad jokes, and he wouldn't be cool about making sandwiches for me and a stranger in the middle of a random school day. He's not all warm and fuzzy and evolved about his feelings.

That's always been his personality, but he withdrew even more after Julian died.

The way I looked up to my brother... that's how Julian looked up to Dad. Sometimes I think it's because they had so many years together before Ida and I came along. They didn't have a lot in common. Dad's never been that involved in activism; he pays attention to politics and he votes, but he'd rather spend a weekend watching sports than holding community meetings. Maybe the bond between them was something inexplicable, something I'd never understand, even if Julian were still here. Maybe it's because my brother was his firstborn.

I once asked Julian if Dad was different when they were alone. If he opened up to him or had a whole arsenal of jokes he was just waiting to unleash on someone.

Julian curled his finger under his chin and pressed his thumb over his lips like he did when he was thinking. Finally he said, "Nah. Not *different*. Just... Here's what I figured out about Dad, little homie."

My brother called me that until the day he died, and it should've bothered me, since he only came up to my shoulder by then, but I dunno. Think I would've missed it if he'd stopped.

"Dad may be a man of few words," Julian continued, "but he's always present."

I snorted. *Present?* "What does that mean?"

Julian tossed a handful of spaghetti noodles into boiling water. It was just the two of us at his apartment that night—the way I liked it best. Having an activist for a brother meant having to share him with a whole lot of people, and sometimes I just wanted him to myself.

He pulled a jar of pasta sauce from the cabinet and plunked it on the counter. "I mean, even when he's just kicking it in his recliner, watching football, he's still there. Paying attention to what's going on around him in the house. Have you ever noticed how he always knows what's up with us, even though Ma was the one who talked to us about it and not him?"

I shrugged. "Yeah, because Ma tells him what we talked about."

"Not always," Julian said, shaking his head. "He's there, Duke. Even if he doesn't seem like it."

But if Dad was quiet before, he pretty much stopped talking after Julian died. He'd answer us when we spoke to him. And lots of days he had it in him to fight with

Ma—and they fought about *everything*: bills, housework, what to do with Julian's stuff. I knew things were pretty much over with them when he didn't even bother to argue back.

I thought he might change for the better when they split up and we moved into the new house, but it seemed kinda worse then. He was alone all the time when Ida and I weren't staying with him, and you could tell. The freezer was filled with boxes of frozen dinners, and the trash piled up with old takeout containers. He didn't date, he didn't see anyone outside of work, and he didn't talk to us about anything real when we were over. Just asked about school and made sure we didn't need money before he went back to the game on TV.

Still, I've never forgotten what Julian said. That under that hard shell, there's something. Someone who cares. I haven't seen that Dad in a minute, but I'll never forget how he helped me at Julian's memorial service. The worst day of my life. Actually, I still haven't been able to figure out if the worst day was the memorial service, the burial, or when he was killed.

I didn't want to speak, but I had to. I was close to him. His little homie. Everyone expected it. Even Ida got up there and said a little something about him.

One of Julian's friends, a girl named Katie or Kayla or something like that, had just walked down the aisle to her seat, sniffling into a tissue, after saying nice words about him. It was my turn, but I couldn't move. Not until Ma touched my shoulder and said, "I'll be right here, sweetheart."

I swallowed hard and stood up, wishing for the millionth time in the past year that I could shrink myself. Or put on an invisible suit. Anything to keep people from staring at me. We were in the front row, so in just a few short steps I was in front of the mic, looking out at everyone who'd come to say good-bye to my brother.

Next to me, there was a blown-up picture of him on display, but no casket. The burial was going to be closed, only for family. This was for everyone else—the community he loved, who loved him back.

I pulled a piece of paper from the pocket of my suit jacket and slowly unfolded it, aware of how much my hands were shaking but unable to stop them. I looked only at the paper. If I didn't make eye contact with anyone or look at that picture of him, maybe I could get through it.

"My brother, Julian, is the best person I know," I said, my voice wobbly on the microphone. "*Was,*" I corrected myself, and there was a collective pause in the audience as the word sank in. I took a deep breath. "He always put everyone else first—his community, his friends, and his family. If someone was in trouble, Julian wanted to help them. He did whatever he could. He—"

My voice broke. I sniffed a couple of times, running the back of my hand across my nose. And I tried to go on, but I couldn't. Every time I opened my mouth, nothing came out. I didn't look at Ma, but I could tell she was leaning forward in her seat, trying to get my attention. I was quiet for so long that people started to murmur. So long that I wondered if I might die up there.

A deep voice—one I didn't recognize—called out, "Go 'head, Duke!"

A woman's voice followed: "You got this, baby!"

I nodded, still staring down at the paper. Trying to continue and failing every time. I shook my head and started folding up my speech, but my eyes filled before I could get away from everyone's gaze. I tried to stand still, thinking maybe the tears would go away if I just froze. But they dripped down my face and onto my collar, and then my shoulders started to shake, and I wasn't fooling anybody.

There was a rustling in the front row, and I guessed Ma finally felt bad enough to come up and get me. Save the last of my dignity, even though I'd probably be known forever as Julian's little brother who couldn't even keep it together long enough to eulogize him.

But then someone jogged up and put their arm around me, and when I raised my head, I saw it was Dad. He leaned in to whisper in my ear, "It's okay. You're gonna be all right. We're gonna get through this, okay? You got this, Duke."

I brushed at my eyes, nodding. It was the most he'd said since Julian had died. And I knew he didn't want to be up there any more than I did. That meant something, too.

I wiped my nose with the sleeve of my suit jacket, took a deep breath, and started again.

Dad stood with me as I read the whole thing, squeezing my shoulder when my voice got shaky.

When I finished, he wrapped his arms around me for what felt like a long time. I couldn't remember the last time my dad had hugged me, and right then, I never wanted him to let me go.

MARVA

WE START SEEING CROWDS OF PEOPLE AS SOON as we get into my neighborhood.

Dozens of people walking together, toward French and Robinson, clearly here to help us find Selma. It makes my heart jump and my breath catch in my throat. I can't believe so many people saw my message and took time out of their day to look for her. I can't believe my little Selma could have such an impact on people. It makes me wonder how many of them decided to vote because of the posts I've been putting on her page during election season.

"You've already got over a thousand comments on your video," Duke says. "People are really into this."

He shows them to me as I park a couple of streets over from mine, down French Street.

My grandbaby loves this cat so we'll be there

Mad respect to you Marva, we got you, be there soon

I'm 2,000 miles away but I'd help if I could

U single girl?

I roll my eyes at the last one, and it's not the only one of its kind, but for the most part, people are being incredibly decent, saying how sorry they are or how they'll tell their friends in the area to stop by if they can or how they know she'll come home soon because her fans will miss her too much. It's sweet to know so many of them care about this cat they've never met. And that they still care now that they know who's behind the account.

People start noticing me the closer we get to the meeting point. Well, I'm pretty sure they notice Duke first. It's easy for him to part the crowd. But once they spot me, everyone starts trying to talk at once, telling me how glad they are to help and wondering what the plan is for the search party.

"What *is* the plan?" Duke asks once we're at the head of the crowd.

And it is a *crowd*. White, Black, Latinx, Asian. Our age, our parents' age, our *grand*parents' age, and babies in strollers. I see people from Salinas Prep I've never even talked to, who are staring at me in awe, as if I'm a completely different person. Some of my neighbors are here, and I spot a couple of my parents' friends in the crowd, too. Even Mrs. Thomas is here, wearing different yoga pants and trying to wrangle her children.

Everyone is looking at me, waiting for me to say something. But for once, I don't have a plan. If I did, I'm not even sure I'd be able to remember it. I don't mind being in front of people when I have to give a presentation in class, or when I'm running a student council meeting. But this . . . I'm not prepared at all. What do I say that I didn't already say on the video? We need to find Selma.

I glance at Duke. "I . . . I don't know."

He pauses, then says, "There's a *lot* of people here, and more keep showing up."

"I *know*," I say, glancing nervously out at the crowd.

"Why don't we see if they can split up? Half can look for Selma, because honestly, that's enough people. Looking for a cat is different from looking for a dog. She'll probably be freaked out at everyone walking around, calling for her. Having so many people doing it at once could backfire."

"Okay, soooo where are the other people going to go?"

I avoid making eye contact with anyone in the crowd, worried they're going to get annoyed and leave if we don't announce a plan soon. But Duke is squinting as he stares off at a point in the distance, and I can tell he's thought of something when he starts nodding and smiling.

"You said you would've taken today off to drive people to the polls if you could have," he says. "Here's our chance."

His eyes are shining, and *this* is the most excited I've seen him all day. Even more excited than when we were eating bologna sandwiches and during our time at the beach. Maybe my commitment to voting is finally rubbing off on him. Or maybe he's cared this much the whole time and wasn't sure what to do with it. Either way, I am loving this side of Duke.

"That's a great idea, but how are we going to organize people to do this?"

If I'm underprepared for once in my life, Duke seems to be completely comfortable taking charge.

"Clive said his senior center organized the bus to go to their original polling place, but then they couldn't all get to the church once they realized the regular spot had been closed up. I could call the senior center to see if they're accepting rides from people. And maybe some other places around town that they know need help. It's last-minute, but maybe it'll work? It's better than nothing," he says.

I stare at him, stunned that such practical words could turn my knees to jelly. It's something I hadn't thought of, and it makes me look at him in a new way.

"Duke, it's everything," I breathe.

The crowd is getting restless, so Duke fires off his big whistle to get everyone's attention. I stand next to him and watch their faces as he tells them the plan. It's a mix of reactions. Some people walk off right away, saying they just came to see what the fuss was all about. Others look less than enthused, but they stay until he's finished talking. But plenty—more than I expected—step up when he says we need drivers. I even notice a few people from Salinas Prep volunteering, and I'm so shocked they'd be willing to offer up their luxury cars to help strangers get to the polls that I am speechless.

Duke handles everything, from telling the search party where, when, and how often to report back, to calling Flores Hills Senior Center so they can work out the details, and posting on the band's page to ask for additional help.

And, for once, I sit back and watch, completely comfortable not being in charge. Completely in awe of how Duke managed to hide this part of himself until now.

Once everyone is organized and dispersed and it's just us, I am suddenly shy. He just stepped up in such a huge way—in such an *unexpected* way—and I don't know what to say.

"How can I ever repay you for this?" I ask, looking up at him.

He shrugs his big shoulders, just as bashful as I feel. "It was a couple of phone calls and some logistics. I didn't do much."

"You did so much, Duke. I . . . I don't know what to say except thank you."

He touches my hand. Softly. Briefly. "Cool. That's enough for me."

DUKE

GOTTA ADMIT, I'M KINDA FEELING MYSELF AS WE walk back to the Volvo.

I didn't do any of that to impress her. *She's* been doing this for months—years now. Everybody needs a break, so when she needed me to step up, I did.

But impressing her is a pretty nice side effect. I don't know the last time someone looked so proud of me.

I'm on top of the world for about five minutes until I come all the way down real quick. Because walking up to us in a line like a goddamn army is my entire family: Ma,

Dad, and Ida, who's heading up the pack and looks like she'd rather be anywhere but here.

Her expression changes from grouchy to excited as soon as she sees who I'm with.

"Oh my god, I can't believe Eartha Kitty is your cat!" Ida exclaims, running up to Marva. "She's my favorite animal on the internet! I told Ma and Dad we had to come down here and look for her."

"Thanks, Ida," Marva says, looking unsure of what to do with my parents here, too. "Everyone has split up. Some people are going to look for her, and the others are going to help drive people to the polls."

"Well, I'm ready to go look for Eartha Kitty. Which way should we go?"

"Actually, her name is—" Marva starts to correct her, but before either of them can get any further, Dad says, "Ida, you're staying with us. We came to see if your brother was here, not to look for some cat."

His words are low and clipped, a sure sign his anger is ready to bubble over at any second. I only need to look at the storm brewing behind his eyes to see how pissed he really is.

Oh, man. This is gonna be bad.

Marva touches my arm. "I'm going to stop in at home

and talk to my dad. I'll meet you back at the Volvo. . . . I mean, if you still want a ride?"

If talking to her was ever awkward before, it's a thousand times worse with my family standing here. Dad's eyes are burning a hole in my head.

"Uh, yeah, sounds like a plan." If my parents don't kill us first.

Once Marva walks away, the four of us just stand there in a circle, looking at one another. I figured Dad would be raring to go, especially since I didn't answer any of his angry texts, but all of a sudden he has nothing to say? His energy is speaking loud enough.

Ma takes the reins. "We don't like knowing that you two are lying to us."

"We didn't lie," Ida says right away. She's standing with her hands clasped together. "You never asked where I was going that day. And it was civil. Nonviolent. Just like Julian used to do."

"You are not Julian," Ma says. "And now you're fifteen years old with an arrest record."

"Yeah, an arrest for standing up for women's rights, Ma! You're a feminist, so you should support a woman's right to choose."

"Ida, this has nothing to do with my stance on abortion.

And, yes, I *am* pro-choice. I'm not mad about what you were protesting. I'm mad that you did it behind our backs when you knew we weren't comfortable with it! Do you know how dangerous these things are? They can end in—"

"Come on, Ma. Civil disobedience has been happening since the beginning of time," Ida says, crossing her arms.

"Don't interrupt your mother." Dad's voice is low and firm. "You know better than this, Ida. It doesn't matter how long people have been protesting—*you* could've still been hurt."

"Did you give the same speeches to Julian when he wanted to support a cause? Or did you just tell him you didn't like it but let him go anyway because he wasn't a girl?" She shakes her head, and I have to give it to my little sis, because she's a lot braver than I would be right now. I'd probably just shut up, take the punishment, and get the hell out of there as fast as I could. She's not letting them win that easily. "I can't live my life for you guys."

"Ida, all we're saying is that we need to talk about these things." Ma's voice is a bit more patient than Dad's, but not much. Her lips are pressed together in such a tight line, I can barely see them. "You can't just decide to go off and get arrested on a Saturday on a whim."

"It *wasn't* a whim. The whole point of a sit-in is to

plan it. And I've tried to talk to you guys about this. A few times, and you won't take me seriously." Ida lets out a breath. "I'm not in the social justice club just because it looks good. I care about changing things. I want to be out there, just like Julian was."

"Julian is dead!" Dad barks, and his words echo around the neighborhood so loudly, I freeze.

We all do.

The anger has officially bubbled over. His face is chiseled into a deep, immovable frown, and he's shaking. I've seen him mad, but I dunno if I've ever seen him *this* mad, and I wonder if he usually hides it from us when it gets like this.

"He's dead, and he might not be if he hadn't been out on the front lines, doing sit-ins and going to protests that *did* get violent and getting involved with people who didn't give a damn whether he lived to see another day!"

Ida swallows hard. "But you can't blame his death on activism, Dad. He might've still been shot if he wasn't involved in any of that."

He has nothing to say to that, so he turns to me.

Shit. My turn.

I hate the look he's giving me. Like he's never been more disappointed.

"And we don't appreciate your role in this, Duke," he says. "You know better than to ferry your sister back and forth to something we wouldn't approve of and bail her out of *jail* without telling us. You're eighteen, but you're still our child. Living under our roofs."

Ida and I make eye contact across the circle. Normally I'd just say *Okay* and *Sorry* and *I won't do it again*. But I can't go out like that, letting my little sis take all the heat and not stand up for her.

"She asked me to help her out," I say, my voice shaky. "I'm her brother. Should I have said no?"

"You should have *talked to us*, dammit!" Dad yells, clenching his hands into fists.

"Charles," Ma says. Just one word, but he snaps his mouth closed and relaxes his fingers.

"Dad, I'm not trying to piss you off, but I gotta say . . ." I swallow and look at Ida again. She gives me the tiniest nod. So small I could've missed it, but it's enough to make me go on. "That's the thing. You're pissed off *all* the time now. It's hard to talk to you about . . . anything."

"He's right," Ida says softly. "I'm not blaming you, but it's been really different since we moved here. Since . . . Julian died. *You've* been different."

Dad stares hard at both of us, his eyes moving from

Ida's face to mine. The storm is still there, and I think we all hold our breaths, wondering how he's going to react to what we've said. I brace myself for an explosion of the worst kind.

But then the air changes. I wonder if it's Julian, watching over us. Maybe his soul is relieved we're finally talking about this. Even if it did take the sister who barely knew him to get it started.

Dad reaches into his pocket and pulls out his wallet. He slips out a small photo and holds it up so we can all see. It's a picture of him and Julian, when my brother was just a baby. Way before Ida or I even got here. Dad's cradling Julian, and they're both staring at each other like they've never seen anyone better. The picture is wrinkly and creased. I wonder how long he's been carrying it around.

"*This* is what I think of when I think of Julian. Him being this little. This dependent on me." His voice is so low I have to strain to catch his words. "And now my baby boy is dead. I couldn't protect him. I gave him that freedom he wanted, but I should've seen that he could never truly be free. And I . . . I'm a Black man. It was *my* job to teach him what that meant in this world, how much more dangerous it was for him, and I failed. I failed him. I'm doing the best I can to protect you two. I'm sorry if my anger is too much for you, but I'm not going to lose another child." He slides the photo back into his wallet.

I swallow. Hard to believe Julian was ever that small and helpless. And I guess part of me knew Dad felt this way, but hearing him say it makes my chest hurt.

I feel an itch creeping up my throat because I know he's not gonna like what I have to say and it might set him off again, but I gotta say it. For Ida and me.

"But your best isn't good enough."

"Duke Benjamin Crenshaw!" Ma says at the same time Dad says, "*Excuse* me?"

"Ma made us go to therapy, and she went, too," Ida says, not missing a beat. "We *all* talked to somebody, except for you. You can't just be okay."

Dad scowls down at the pavement. "People process things differently. Talking about it doesn't make me feel better."

"But you don't talk to *anybody*." My sister bites her lip. "Not me or Duke or Ma."

"Ida, you need to stay out of grown folks' business," he says, his eyebrows pinched tight. "I'm your father, not your friend."

"Dad, it's true." I crack a couple of knuckles, almost

afraid to look at him. But I do. "I don't know how to talk to you anymore. You're not the same person."

"None of us are the same person, Duke." He doesn't meet my eyes, but I can tell the storm in his is fading. His voice sounds like it's lost some of the fight, too.

"I know." I nod. "I think about him all the time. I miss the hell out of him."

Ma doesn't even yell at me for cursing, and when I look at her, she's blinking rapidly, her eyes damp.

I take a deep breath. I can't believe how much I'm talking right now, especially saying things I know are going to piss him off. But... if not now, when?

"Dad... telling Ida to give up activism is like telling me to give up drums at this point. It's too late. She's already an activist. It's what she believes in. It's her therapy, helping people. Just like music is mine."

Ida stares at me, surprised. I'm surprised at myself, too, but I go on.

"That's what people want—for us to be too scared to stand up for ourselves and what we believe in. I think that's more dangerous than trying to change things. Julian wouldn't want you to keep her on a tight leash. He'd want his little sister to show people that she was just as tough as he was."

Dad doesn't say anything. But his breathing looks like it's going back to normal instead of the quick, short breaths he was taking earlier, and that's gotta be good.

"We're not unreasonable," Ma says, pushing a piece of hair behind her ear. "But what if something had happened, Ida? You're growing up, but you're not grown yet. And I *am* a feminist, but you're my daughter. I can't stop myself from worrying about you."

"I just don't want to be treated like a baby," Ida says. "I want to be able to express myself. Like Duke said, this is me. I'm not doing it because I think it's trendy or makes me look good. It feels like something I can't *not* do."

Dad shakes his head, but he doesn't look pissed anymore. Well, not *so* pissed. "All three of you kids are so damn hardheaded."

"Gee, I wonder what the common denominator is?" Ida says, looking back and forth between him and Ma.

"Look, we can talk about this." Ma briefly touches each of our shoulders. "If you promise not to keep any more secrets from us, we'll sit down and have a real conversation about all the ways you can get involved. Pros and cons. All of it. Maybe we can call up some of Julian's old friends and see what advice they have. This doesn't mean you can run off to whatever protest or demonstration that you want, because you are still fifteen years old. But we can talk."

"Yes," Dad says slowly. "We can talk."

Ida nods. "That sounds good."

Ma looks at me. "And no more covering up for your sister."

"Okay," I reply. I think that's a promise I can keep, as long as they keep their promise to talk to us about things.

She looks around the neighborhood as if she's just seeing it for the first time. "Now, whose cat is it that brought us out here?"

"Mar-va," Ida says in a singsongy voice. "Duke's new *friend.*"

Ma eyes me. "The girl you're skipping school with today?"

"We didn't technically skip school, Ma. I mean, not on purpose."

"We can talk about that later, too," she says, eyebrow raised.

Ma and Dad step away a few feet to talk.

"That was . . . not what I expected," Ida says, watching them walk off together.

"Yeah, me either. You okay?"

She nods. "I think so. What about you?"

"I'm okay. I'm good." And I am.

"You should go for Marva," she blurts.

"What?"

"Marva! You should totally go for her. She's a little uptight, but she's supersmart. And kind of funny, even if it's mostly online. I mean, some of those Eartha Kitty posts are *genius*."

I stuff my hands in my pockets. "She's funny in person, too. But she just broke up with her boyfriend."

Ida purses her lips, looking just like Ma. "Wait, when? Like, *today*? After you'd been hanging out? Duke, that has to mean something!"

"It doesn't mean anything except that today is the day they broke up. Besides, who says I like her?"

"Uh, literally every part of your body language?"

I shake my head. "Stop making shit up. We're just . . ."

What? Friends? Can you become friends with someone in a matter of hours, or is that still an acquaintance? Kendall and I became friends pretty quickly, but that was different. There was a computer screen and then a phone screen between us.

"You're totally into her," Ida says.

I throw up my hands. "Even if I was, what am I gonna do about it? I can't just ask her out right after they broke up."

"Well, who broke up with *whom*?"

"I don't know. I wasn't there. I just know he pulled up, saw us together, and when I got back to the car, they were broken up."

"He *saw* you together?" Ida's face lights up like an arena. This is probably the greatest thing that's happened to her in weeks, and it has nothing to do with her.

I clear my throat. "It's not like that. We were just walking. Talking."

"Mm-hmm." Ida can't stop grinning. "Well, I think you should keep in touch with her so you can be together when it *is* appropriate to ask her out."

I laugh. "You are *trippin'*, sis."

She bats her eyelashes at me. "You love it."

"That all you need to bug me about? I gotta get going so I can vote and warm up for my show."

"Well..." Her foot traces a swirly pattern on the sidewalk. "I just wanted to say thanks. For going with me, and bailing me out, and talking to Ma and Dad, and... you know, everything. You're a good big brother."

Well, damn. Sure wasn't expecting this. It makes my ears hot when people say nice things about me.

"Yeah, it's cool, Ida." I shrug. "Gotta step up since it's just the two of us."

"You were always there," she says, tilting her head to the side. "You know that, right? Even before Julian was gone. I know he was, like, the world to you, but..." She pauses, glancing down at the ground before she looks at me again. "That's what you are to me."

Wow. It's amazing how someone you want to kill half the time can also say something that makes your throat get all lumpy.

"Even though I'm not like Julian at all?"

"That's the point, knucklehead," she says, flicking me on the arm. "You are who you're supposed to be."

A smile turns up the corner of my mouth. "Someone pay you to say that?"

She points her chin at me. "No, and if you ever tell anyone, I'll deny it forever."

I bend down and give her a hug—something we almost never do. "You're not so bad yourself, little sis. Love you."

Marva shows up at her car ten minutes later, looking so gloomy that I frown as I get in.

"Any news about Selma?"

"Nothing new. The search party is posting about it and taking pictures of where they've been, but nobody's seen her yet." She pulls away from the curb, steering us back into the world for what seems like the hundredth time today. “How was your family meeting?”

“Good. Productive, I think? Ida and I are still alive, anyway.”

“That *is* productive. Ida’s okay?”

“Yeah, she is.” I smile. “I’ll tell her you asked.”

She nods. “Thanks.” Then: “So, we are finally, totally, *definitely* on our way to vote. Do you need anything before we go? You have your ID, right?”

I pat my wallet in the back pocket of my jeans. “Got it.” My drumsticks are in my lap. My kit is at Anthony’s, where we practice, so I’ve got everything I need for now. I clear my throat. “I know you got better things to do, but our show is at eight if you wanna come.”

She doesn’t say anything for what feels like forever and that makes me wish *I’d* never said anything. I’m wondering when someone is gonna finally invent a contraption that swallows you from your seat and shoots you into a portal far, far away to get you out of embarrassing situations when she says, “That sounds fun. Are you nervous?”

Only when I think about you being there.

“Usually, but today? Not really. We’ve practiced a lot, so we’ve kinda done all we can do, you know? Rest is up to the performance gods.”

She nods like this makes total sense, and then we're both quiet as she drives toward the church. The silence is good, though. Chill. Like we're definitely friends and not just acquaintances.

The green light ahead changes to yellow when we're just a few yards from the intersection, and Marva puts her foot on the gas to speed through it, same as she's done a half dozen times today.

But this time, there's a whoop of a siren behind us. This time, there's flashing lights.

My stomach lurches.

And this time, Marva looks in the rearview mirror, her eyes wide as she says, "Fuck. We're getting pulled over."

I look in the mirror on my side of the Volvo. See the cop car slowing behind Marva's as she pulls off to the side of the road. I look around. We're on a major street. But I keep peering at the mirror, not brave enough—stupid enough?—to turn around. And all I can see is the cop pressing the radio to their mouth in the front seat.

My hands shake and my throat goes dry as sand.

I'm gonna throw up.

ABOUT JULIAN, PART 2.

OUR DAD GAVE JULIAN THE TALK WHEN HE WAS seven, the same year that I was born.

My brother never did grow as tall as me, but he'd always been a big kid. Always looked older than his age. Dad told him that people would look at him as older, no matter his size. That, to a lot of people, Black boys never really get to be boys. He told Julian that if he was stopped by a cop, by foot or by car, he was to never talk back. That, if he was on foot, he should keep his hands up and in clear view, away from his pockets; if he was in a car, he should keep his hands on the steering wheel or dashboard unless explicitly directed to reach for his license and registration—and that he should do whatever it took to stay alive.

Not safe. *Alive.*

I know this because Julian gave me the same talk, seven years later.

"You my little homie, but you a big dude, Duke," he said. "Tall for your age."

We were shooting hoops at the park, because back then, even at the age of seven, everyone swore I was gonna be a basketball star. I liked playing, especially when Julian let me hoop with him and his friends, but I didn't love it.

"So?" I said, shooting the ball to him.

"*So?*" He shot it back at me fast. Too fast. The ball looked like it was gonna bounce right up and hit me under the chin, and I jumped out of the way.

Julian shook his head, jerking his thumb toward the runaway ball. "Go get that." When I dribbled it back to him, he said, "People gonna look at you different. Like you're older than you are. Like you've done things."

I didn't get it. "What kinda things?"

"Bad things. Things Black men and boys get blamed for all the time, even if they didn't do them."

"Like not taking out the trash?" I couldn't think of anything worse than Ma yelling at me when I forgot to take out the garbage.

Julian sighed, dribbling the ball in place. "Worse, okay? Way worse. So you gotta listen to me when I tell you what to do if a cop ever stops you."

"Why would a cop stop me?"

He wiped sweat from his brow with his nondribbling hand. "Because... sometimes they think bad things about us, even if they don't know us."

"But why would they think that?"

"That's a real long story, little homie. Hundreds of years long. You just need to know what to do now, okay?"

And he went through the rules. One by one. Then he quizzed me.

I told him I'd do what he said, and I memorized his instructions, but I didn't know why he was being so serious. I was seven. And he seemed so old to me then, but he was only fourteen. He couldn't even drive.

But two years later, he *could* drive. And I was in the car with him when he got stopped not a month after he'd gotten his license.

He swore under his breath and, eyes flicking back and forth from the road to the rearview mirror, slowly pulled us to the side. We weren't too far from our house. The car didn't stop rolling until it was a few feet in front of the entrance to a gas station. People were pumping gas and filling the air in their tires and running into the station for snacks and lottery tickets.

I was nine by then. I knew more than I'd known two years ago, but I didn't realize until I was older that Julian was making sure we were as close to a highly visible spot as possible. Where people would see us if anything happened.

The police officer took his time getting out of the car, and Julian sat stock-still, hands clamped to the steering wheel.

"Don't say a *word*," he muttered from the side of his mouth. "I got this."

But he didn't look like it.

I stared straight ahead like Julian, even when the officer tapped on the window and asked him to roll it down. Julian's left hand reached slowly for the automatic window button. He pressed it until the glass was all the way down, letting in a blast of warm July air.

"Evening, boys," the officer said, craning his neck to see who all was in the car. I could feel his eyes on me before they went back to my brother. "Where you headed?"

I frowned. Why was that any of his business? It was

a free country, wasn't it? My tongue itched to say so, but I hadn't forgotten Julian's instructions: *Never talk back.*

"Home, Officer," Julian said, turning his head just slightly toward him. His hands were still on the steering wheel, gripping it tight. "We live a few blocks east of here, off Williams Avenue."

"Mmm. License and registration, please."

Shouldn't he have said why he stopped us? Was Julian speeding? Hadn't seemed like it. Julian didn't like to drive fast anyway. I pressed my tongue against the backs of my teeth.

Felt like it took a hundred years for Julian to grab his wallet and pull out his ID. He handed it to the officer, then said in a clear voice, "Just reaching for my registration." His arm stretched across me in the passenger seat to open the glove box. His hand was shaking, and his fingers trembled as he rifled through the compartment for the car registration.

I'd never seen my brother so freaked. And I hated it. He was always the calmest, most confident person in the room. But right now? I barely recognized him.

I took this opportunity to look over at the officer. His head was still tilted so he could watch Julian. He was younger than I figured he'd be. Or maybe it was just his baby face, with chubby cheeks and wide blue eyes. My gaze quickly slid down to where his hand rested on his hip, inches away from his gun.

I felt sick.

The car was so quiet I heard Julian swallow as his fingers finally found the piece of paper he was looking for. He gave it to the officer and sat straight up in his seat, hands back on the steering wheel.

The officer took Julian's ID and the paper to his car. I looked in the passenger mirror, watching as he sat half in, half out of the driver's side, talking on his radio.

"Why did he—" I began, but Julian's voice cut through mine in an instant.

"Shut. Up."

I did.

The officer came back after what felt like an hour but was only about four minutes when I dared to glance at the clock on the dashboard. Julian hadn't moved.

He gave my brother the paper and driver's license. "Get that taillight fixed," was all he said before he sauntered back to his car, whooped his siren one more time, and sped off.

Julian's body collapsed into the seat, like all his bones were gone.

"Julian?"

He shook his head, eyes closed.

I looked over at the gas station. It was still full of movement, same as before. I wondered if anyone had noticed the cop pull us over. Nobody was even looking our way.

After a moment, Julian swore again and turned on the ignition, car still in park. He threw off his seat belt and jumped out of the driver's side, stalking to the back of the car. I turned around to look at him. He was inspecting the car, looking from left to right. Again and again.

When he got back in, he buckled his seat belt. Ran a hand over his face. When he turned to look at me, his eyes were red.

"Ain't nothing wrong with that taillight. I just checked it last night. That asshole stopped me because he could."

I just looked at him. Now that it was safe to talk, my mouth felt like it was full of marbles.

"This shit happens *all* the time. And we were lucky. He could've said I looked like a suspect and I would've been on the ground in a second. He—" Julian's voice was so thick that it broke. He slammed the heel of his hand against the steering wheel. "This shit has gotta stop."

He didn't say anything else. A few moments later, he put the car into gear and drove us home. When we parked in front of the house, I opened my door to get out, but he just sat there. I saw a tear fall down his cheek, then another one, and another.

"Julian?"

"Little homie, don't you *ever* forget what I told you, okay? You do *exactly* what I did back there."

"Is this gonna happen to me?"

He let out a long, shuddering breath and put his hand on the back of my neck. He didn't answer me, and I didn't ask again.

MARVA

MY PARENTS TOLD ME A LONG TIME AGO WHAT to do if I ever got pulled over by a police officer.

They sat me down together and told me that while a lot of cops are good and doing their best to look out for the community, all the stories about the bad officers were very true. And that I should know some of them will look at me differently because I'm Black, and treat me unfairly. They told me that I had to be polite, obedient, and calm. Do my best to make sure things didn't escalate, even though that wasn't my responsibility.

I remember all of that as the officer walks up to my car. The window is already half-open, and when the cop leans down to look in, I see it's a Latina officer. I swallow. That makes me feel better. A little.

"How are you today?" she asks. Her badge says GONZALEZ.

"Fine, Officer."

"In a hurry?" Her voice is not exactly mean, just... brusque. "I pulled you over because I saw you run that red light."

I thought I made it through before it turned red, but I know better than to argue.

"We're on our way to vote," I say, nodding toward Duke. "Well, I've already voted. I'm driving him."

"The polls are open until eight. You have time," she says. "License and registration?"

I carefully pull out my ID from my bag. My hand brushes against Duke's knee as I reach into the glove compartment for the registration. He's ramrod straight in the seat, eyes focused on the windshield.

Officer Gonzalez looks at my ID and registration for almost a minute, staring from me to the picture on my license several times. She finally hands it back, and says,

"Letting you off with a warning. Look, I get how important voting is, but you have to be careful. No election is worth endangering your life or someone else's, okay?"

"Yes, Officer. Thank you," I say in my most respectful voice. "I promise to be more careful."

She nods at me, and my breath catches when she looks at Duke. *Please don't ask him to get out. Please.*

She pauses, her eyes moving back and forth between us, then says, "You kids have a good night. Be safe."

Duke doesn't breathe until she's back in her car. I don't think he moved once after I pulled over.

I look at him. "Are you okay?"

He swallows, glancing at the Mexican restaurant beside us. The Volvo is a few feet from the entrance. "I keep wondering how many times I'll be so lucky."

"Lucky?"

"The first time I was in a car that got pulled over, my brother said we were lucky. Because the cop didn't make him get out and... he wasn't violent. But I was with him when he got stopped again, two more times. And I've been pulled over and—some people aren't so lucky, you know? Some people don't make it out of a 'routine traffic stop,'" he says, making air quotes with his fingers.

"*This* is why getting people out to vote is so important to me," I say quietly. "We shouldn't still be dealing with this. We never should've *had* to deal with this. Too many people risked their lives and—I'll never forget the first time I heard about the four girls in Birmingham. I was in fifth grade . . . the youngest was the same age as me when she died. Or the Freedom Summer murders. I didn't understand how anyone could hate Black people so much *just* because we were Black." I take a deep breath. "But that's when I learned about people like Bayard Rustin and Diane Nash and Stokely Carmichael and Coretta Scott King and . . . *so many people* who worked over the last century to make sure we wouldn't still be where we are. I know voting doesn't solve everything, and people may think one vote isn't all that important, but I really believe it makes a difference."

I know I'm preaching to the choir, but I want him to understand why I'd willingly spend a whole day running around with someone I barely know. . . . Except, is that still true? Because ever since he got back in my car, it's been hitting me how very comfortable I am with him. Spending today with Duke hasn't felt like a chore. It's been . . . nice.

Then, before I know it, my hand is sliding across the

seat to his. I place my palm over the hand clasped to his knee, and leave it there. He looks down, startled at the sudden warmth of my fingers on his, then his gaze shifts to me.

I've seen other people have conversations with their eyes. I've watched as they work out whole discussions with nothing more than a few blinks and intense stares. But I've never had that with anyone, not even Alec. Not until now.

Because Duke's eyes are telling a story. They are saying that he likes my hand there, and he wishes I would leave it. But that I can't, because that might lead to something else, and *that* can't happen, because I just broke up with my boyfriend. They are saying that he is trying to be good and respectful, but there is something between us, and we both know it.

Yes, my eyes say back. *I know it.*

I pull my hand away and look straight ahead. "Okay, what's going to be our next crisis?"

"Huh?" His voice sounds too loud in the car after what was just unspoken.

"Well, my gas tank is three-quarters full, so we won't run out of that. What else? A flat tire? A fire? A collision?"

"Hey, don't even be joking like that. We'll get there,"

he says. "If that traffic stop was lucky, maybe our luck is turning."

"Yeah, maybe," I say.

And if that's true, I hope Selma is part of that good luck, too.

DUKE

MY STOMACH DROPS AS SOON AS WE PULL UP TO the church.

If it was bad before, the parking lot is an absolute nightmare now. It's dark out, so everything looks even more dramatic under the parking-lot lights. Cars are blocking one another in and people are honking and nobody seems to be getting anywhere. And when I look back at the front of the church, the line is longer than ever.

"Holy shit," Marva breathes as she takes in the scene, too. "Is this because of us?"

"Maybe?"

As we look around, I see a lot of people about Clive's age and even older. Some are just being dropped off before their drivers head out to pick up more people. But others are being escorted up to the church, and some volunteers are even staying to talk with them.

Marva parks in a red zone, saying she'll deal with the ticket later if it comes to that. "We have to go—what time do you need to be at the venue?"

I check the time. I needed to meet up with the band about an hour ago to start getting our gear together. They'll probably be getting to the Fractal in the next half hour, then warm-ups, then . . . damn.

I don't know if anyone was more excited than me about our first paying gig. Drumming has helped keep my head together since Julian died, but I like performing, too. And proving we're good enough to be paid . . . Well, Drugstore Sorrow is one of the dopest things I've ever been a part of, and my stomach sinks when I realize I may not be there for our biggest night yet.

"I don't know if I'm gonna make it," I say, staring at the line. It's just too long. Even if they don't run out of ballots by the time we get to the front, the show will have started long before that.

Except I'm the drummer and they can't go on without me.

Oh, man. I just realize I didn't even check in with the group chat to update them on where I am. They are going to *kill me.*

"But those shows don't ever start on time, do they?" Marva says, eyeing the crowd with me. I see a few of the same faces from before. I wonder if everyone who had to leave earlier made it back. After all we've been through, I hope so. I especially hope Clive already made it in.

"It's all right," I say as we start walking toward the back of the line. "They'll hate me for a little bit, but this won't be our last show. They'll get it once the election results come in. Either way, they'll know this was too important for me to just take off."

"Okay, but, Duke, your *gig* is important, too! You shouldn't have to choose between that and voting." Marva's voice is so loud that people are starting to look at us. "If the people in charge of this had their shit together in any way, you already would've voted this afternoon!"

I'm kinda embarrassed that she's being so loud, but I like that she cares so much. That she realizes the gig and my music *are* important.

"It's okay, Marva. Sometimes things just don't work out. I—"

"Young man? Hey, young man!"

I look up and over at the familiar voice. He's shadowed under the building lights, but I recognize the outline of him and his cane. "Clive?"

"Hey, come on over here!"

Marva and I look at each other before we head over to Clive. He's just a couple of people behind the entrance.

"You're still here?" I ask.

"Still standing," he grumbles. "Was wondering if you'd be back."

"Did they ever deliver the ballots?" Marva glances nervously toward the church.

"Just about twenty minutes ago. A damn mess! But they finally got 'em and they letting us in. Thank god, 'cause people started showing up in *droves* all of a sudden. Someone said some nice kids organized rides for my friends at the senior center. And someone even brought waters and granola bars when they heard how long we'd been waiting."

"That was Duke," Marva says proudly, looking up at me. "He organized the whole thing."

"It was a group effort," I mumble.

"Made possible because of *his* idea."

Clive nods at me, his eyes glistening with respect. "You done good, young man."

"Thank you," I say. "We should get in line now, though. I'm already late to be somewhere."

Or maybe I should stop pretending I'm gonna get to the gig on time. It's not gonna happen.

Clive shakes his head. "You trying to go to the back of the line? After all you've done today to help people? Boy, you better get in line ahead of me. I can't do much, but I can do that for you."

"Oh, no, it's okay, I—"

Marva nudges me. Hard. "Thank you, Clive. We really appreciate it."

"My pleasure," he says, stepping back so we can file in ahead of him. "Y'all a real cute couple. I *love* to see Black love."

Marva grins. So do I.

We don't correct him.

MARVA

HE VOTED.

After all that we've been through—cutting school and disappearing cats and family meetings and broken relationships—Duke got his ballot in.

And with just enough time to get to the Fractal.

"I can call a car," he says once we're in the parking lot again. "It's late, and I know you probably want to get back home to look for Selma."

Yes, part of me wants that. But another part—a *big* part—wants to spend as much time with him as possible.

"There are so many people still looking for her," I say

slowly. "Does it make me a bad cat mom if I don't join them?"

"Nobody I know deserves a break more than you," he says.

My phone buzzes. I look at the screen, my eyes widening as a new text comes in. "My dad says somebody thinks they saw her. At the house behind ours. He's going to keep me posted."

"So . . . do you wanna come to the show?" Duke asks.

"If you don't mind me being there."

He smiles down at me with such warmth it's startling. "I can't imagine you *not* being there."

My skin is the best kind of hot right now.

DUKE

THE BAND IS FUCKING PISSED.

To be fair, I would be, too. I've been MIA all day, I left them to deal with my gear, and now I'm showing up fifteen minutes before we're supposed to go on.

"Where the hell have you *been*?" Svetlana glares at me as I stand in the doorway of the Fractal's dressing room, which is really more of a converted storage closet with a table and a couple of chairs.

"Dude, you will never believe this day, and honestly, I don't have enough time to tell you before we go on," I say, running a hand over my head.

"You missed the sound check, man," Anthony says, shaking his head at me. "Not cool."

"I know. I'm sorry, guys. For real. I feel like I've been all over town in the last twelve hours."

Benicio shakes his shaggy hair out of his eyes. "I saw your sister at lunch. She said you were running around with some girl."

I twirl my sticks in my hand, trying to warm up my wrists. "She's not just some girl. She's pretty amazing, actually, and she made sure I got to—"

"Cool story, but you guys need to get out there." The voice comes from behind me, and I turn around to see Kendall standing in the hall. "The Fractal doesn't mess around with their acts. We've only got thirty minutes as the opener. They want the headliner set up with their gear and ready to play by nine."

"Okay," I say. "I'm ready."

I don't know if that's true. We've practiced so much, I feel like I am. But when Marva asked me about our songs on the way over here, I couldn't name one. What if I forget everything we've been working on? And in front of the girl I've liked more than anyone in . . . maybe ever?

They file out of the dressing room, brushing past me one by one, faces stony.

"I hope she's cute," Svetlana huffs as she passes.

Kendall starts to follow them, but I say, "Hey, Kendall. Wait."

She stops but doesn't turn around. Her back is stiff and straight.

"I'm sorry," I say. "I mean, for being late, but also . . ."

"You've already said that. You don't need to keep apologizing. I get it, okay? You liked me better when I was just a person behind a keyboard, not the actual person. End of story."

I inhale. "But does it have to be the end of our story?"

She glares at me. "What are you talking about?"

"You've been a good friend to me, Kendall. Like not a lot of people have. You understand me and my life and everything with Julian like no one else I've met. I guess . . . that's important to me. Your friendship . . . it's important."

"Then why did you say that, Duke?" Her eyes are dry but they show the hurt that's built up since that night at the party. "It was embarrassing. Like, what did that even mean, that you liked it better when we only knew each other online? You don't want to be seen with me? You liked me better when you didn't have to hear my voice?"

I wince. I still can't believe I said that, and I can't blame it all on the vodka.

"No. God, no. Kendall. I didn't mean... Look, you helped me so much after Julian died, and I don't even know how to thank you for that, for real." I pause. Tell myself to take the time to get the words right instead of blurting out whatever will get me out of here the fastest. "I think what I was trying to say was that it was easier for me to talk about that stuff online. You brought up Ethan, and asked me about Julian and... I got nervous. I wasn't used to showing that part of myself to anyone in person."

"But we've been friends for *years* now, Duke. Did you really think we'd never talk about it?" She twists her hands at her sternum. "I noticed that you never brought up Julian when we hung out, so I didn't either. But then I started wondering why. And... are you ashamed of what happened to our brothers?"

I flinch. I deserve that, but damn. I'd *never* be ashamed of Julian. "No, of course not. I... I guess I'm just used to people looking at me a certain way when I talk about him. They assume things."

"So let them assume!" she says. "My brother wasn't perfect, but he was my brother. And I loved him. And it's okay that people know that. It's okay to talk about it. About him."

She's right. Worrying about what other people think

isn't gonna change what happened. Talking about my feelings in front of her, in person—that doesn't make me a loser. It's real life.

"I'm sorry, Kendall." She starts to talk again, but I hold up my hand. "That's the last time I'll say it, okay? But what I said that night was shitty. And I don't want to wreck what we've got. I'm not saying I'm gonna be perfect or, like, suddenly cool about pouring my guts out to you in person. But I'll try to get better."

She looks at me for a bit, then takes a long, deep breath. "Promise?"

"Promise," I say.

Kendall appraises me, arms crossed. "Okay. Now we really have to get out there or the stage manager is going to kill us."

"Hey, Kendall?" I say before she turns around.

"Yeah?"

"We're good? For real?"

"Yeah, Duke," she says with a small smile. "We're good."

The curtain is still closed when we get to the stage and the band is already positioned in their respective places:

Anthony behind the keyboard, Svetlana by the mic with her guitar strapped over her front, and Benicio in the corner, hugging his bass. I slide onto the stool behind my kit, sticks in hand.

"You all ready?" the stage manager, a small kid with frizzy black hair, asks. "Don't forget, it needs to be a tight thirty. We'll cut your sound if we have to."

Kendall wasn't kidding about this guy. But we just nod. I think we're all still in shock that they're paying us, so we'll do whatever the hell they say. It's not a lot of money or anything—barely enough for each of us to buy lunch. But it's something. It means we're legit.

"Hey, everybody!" the stage manager says on the other side of the curtain, addressing the crowd. "Thanks for coming out tonight! We've got the amazing headlining band, the Ashen Nobles, which will be going on in just a few. But first, please help us welcome to the Fractal stage for the very first time—Drugstore Sorrow!"

The audience cheers, and when the curtain snaps up, I can't see a thing. The stage lights are too bright from my seat behind the kit. I can hear people and make out general dark shapes, outlines of bodies, but I don't recognize anyone. And maybe that's better, because I know Marva is out there, and I don't want to be able to watch her face, seeing what she thinks of us in real time. I should've played her one of our practice sessions so she wouldn't be surprised.

But it's too late to worry about that. It's too late to do anything but crack my knuckles, flex my wrists, and count us off to start the show. I tap my sticks together: *One, two, one-two-three-four...*

We start off with what Svetlana calls our shit-kicking-est song. It's fast on the beat, my sticks getting a serious workout on the snare, and it always gets people dancing. Svetlana's voice wails at just the right pitch, Anthony's fingers work like magic over the keys, and Benicio is jamming the fuck out of that bass. We sound good, and I am so damn relieved. I'd never hear the end of it if we didn't; I'm well aware that if anything goes wrong tonight, I'll be taking all the blame.

Our second song is our most experimental one, with me keeping a soft, slow beat that starts out heavy on the hi-hat, letting Benicio's bass take the lead. My eyes have adjusted a little to the lights, but I still can't see anyone out in the crowd. I do see movement, though, so I hope that means people are into it.

By the time our fourth and final song is up, I'm soaked

with sweat and high on adrenaline. Random whoops burst out from the crowd just often enough to energize us and keep us going. Anthony's rhymes are fire, Svetlana's backup singing is the perfect balance, and we're all in sync. You'd never know they all wanted to kill me before we started our set. And I never want to stop.

But the song eventually winds down, and we play the final notes, and the audience is going wild, cheering and even chanting our name: "Drugstore Sorrow! Drugstore Sorrow!" I look at Anthony, wiping my forearm across my face. He grins back at me, and I'm pretty sure all will be forgiven by tomorrow.

As soon as the curtain goes down, we start screaming and jumping around, hugging and talking over one another.

"We fucking *did* that," I whoop, not caring who hears us on the other side of the curtain.

"Guys, we kicked so much ass," Svetlana breathes, her red-lipped mouth open wide in a smile.

"Wasn't sure we were gonna do it, but we totally pulled that off," Anthony says, shaking his head. He knocks me with his elbow. "No thanks to you."

"Credit where it's due, Ant." Svetlana eyes me. "He

was a real shit, disappearing today like he did, but Duke held his own on those drums."

"Dope," Benicio says, his hair falling into his eyes.

"We need you and your gear out of here, like, yesterday," the stage manager says, watching us with his hands on his hips.

"He is *such* a bitch," Svetlana murmurs, but she gives him a sickly sweet smile as we begin disassembling our things. Kendall runs from backstage to help us, and she keeps saying how good we were. She looks proud. Our eyes catch across the stage and she gives me a small nod.

I can't help wondering what Marva thought. Even if she doesn't like it, I hope she knows that was the best we've ever done. Seems like everyone in that room had to feel it. Anthony pulls the van up to the back entrance and we start loading in our things. I'm carrying as much as I can without dropping it, because I just want to get out there as fast as I can and see Marva.

As soon as we're done, I tell the band I'll catch them inside and sprint around the building to come in the front door. The place is *packed*. I'm glad I couldn't see anything from the stage, because I don't think I would've been able to play if I'd known how many people were actually watching us.

One advantage of being as tall as I am is I can see over the tops of most people's heads. Makes finding someone in a crowd pretty easy. Like now, when I spot Marva standing off to the side of the juice bar with my sister. I got a text from Ida right before the band went on, saying our parents were so exhausted after our family meeting that they didn't protest when she asked to come tonight. Dad dropped her off and everything. I think he and Ma are just happy she's being honest with them. Ida and Marva are laughing and talking like they've known each other for years, and it kind of makes me nervous how much they like each other. Ida knows too much about me.

I fan myself with my shirt, but I'm so sweaty, the only thing that's going to help is a long, hot shower. I hope Marva doesn't mind.

When Ida sees me coming, she breaks out into a grin and nudges Marva. "Make way for the rock star!"

"Shut it," I say, shaking my head.

"You guys were really, really good, Duke," my sister says. "For real."

"Thanks, Ida." I look at Marva, who's watching me

with an unreadable expression. "If you hated it, you can pretend like you don't know me."

"The only thing I hated was that you didn't play longer! Duke, Drugstore Sorrow is totally good!"

My ears start to flame. "You don't have to say it to make me feel better. I know we're probably not your thing."

"Stop being a diva and take the compliment."

I shove my hands into my pockets. "Thanks."

Ida is looking at her phone. "Mom wants to know if we'll be home soon. The election results are starting to roll in."

Marva looks sick.

"Are you gonna watch?" I ask.

"Yeah, of course. I need to do it at home, though. I want to be there if Selma comes back."

"They still haven't found her?"

"Not yet," she says, her eyes sad and tired.

"I'm sorry," I say. "I really thought with all those people, they'd be able to find her."

"Yeah, me too." She pauses. "Do you want to come over to watch the results? We started this day together, so it only seems right that we end it that way."

"Yeah," I say. "I'll come over and watch with you."

Ida is looking back and forth between us with the biggest grin. The human equivalent of the heart-eyes emoji.

And it kind of grosses me out that she's looking at us like that, but when my eyes land on Marva . . . well, I gotta admit, I feel the same way.

MARVA

WE GET BACK TO MY HOUSE AROUND NINE THIRTY after we drop off Ida.

"Your parents know I'm coming, right?" he asks, looking up at the house nervously.

"I texted them," I say, pulling my backpack out of the backseat. "They're cool with it. My mom's just about as chill as my dad."

He stops me before I can walk past him toward the house. "Wait."

I look at him expectantly.

"Thank you. For everything you did for me today. You were . . . you *are* fucking amazing, Marva Sheridan."

I give him a tired smile. "You don't have to thank me. I didn't do anything I didn't want to do. But . . . Duke. What if it's not enough? If it was so hard for you and the rest of the people at the church to vote today, think about other people. The ones who gave up when they weren't on the voting roll or their polling place was closed . . ."

I trail off. If I keep talking, I might disappear in a cloud of anxiety. Duke touches my shoulder and lightly squeezes.

"Well, I made it. Clive made it. And so did a bunch of his friends," he says. "I have to think other people realized how important this is and figured it out, too. Even if they weren't lucky enough to have a Marva Sheridan on their side. There's nothing more you could've done to impact this election except run for office yourself. And I have a feeling it's just a matter of time until that happens. . . ."

I tip my face up. Duke is haloed by the white of the streetlight, and his face has never looked better.

For as long as I can remember, I've planned out my entire life. I've had rules about what I am going to do and when, who belongs in my life and doesn't, what I care about and don't. But today has been the biggest surprise of my eighteen years. When I met Duke, I never imagined we'd end up here. And even if the breakup with Alec is new, wanting to kiss Duke is real.

"I like you," I whisper, hoping the words don't get lost in the cool night air.

He rubs my back and his eyes smile down at me as he says, "I like you, too. What are we gonna do about it?"

"This, I think." I rise up on my tiptoes and he bends down to meet me and—

This. Kiss. Is. Perfect. Truly, it's as if our mouths were meant to fit together. His thick lips are warm against mine, and he tugs my bottom one between his teeth, nibbling gently before he pulls away.

"God, I've been wanting to do that for a minute," he says, smiling. He traces my lips with his finger, drawing a slow, careful line that makes me shiver.

I stare at him the whole time, watching the way his eyes crinkle as he examines every inch of my face, as if he's just seeing me for the first time. We kiss again, our mouths opening. His tongue is soft as it gently explores mine, and he tastes fresh, like mint, and I never want this to stop, and—

I pull away with no warning. "What was that?"

"The best thing that's happened to me today?" he says in a lazy voice.

"No, it sounded like—"

There it is again.

A meow.

And when I look around Duke's broad form, there, sitting in the middle of the driveway, is my Selma. Tail wrapped around herself and blinking at me like butter wouldn't melt in her mouth.

"Oh my god! You're home!" I race over to her before she has a chance to get away and scoop her up, smushing my face into her soft, soft fur. "Oh, Selma, I *missed* you."

She meows again, squirming in my arms, but I hold tight.

"Damn," Duke says, following us up to the front door. "I can't believe I'm in the presence of *the* Eartha Kitty."

"Mom, Dad!" I call out as soon as I step into the brightly lit living room. "Selma's home!"

They appear from the back of the house, both wearing their pajamas. Dad looks thrilled to see Duke is back—maybe even more thrilled than he is to see Selma.

"Where'd you find her?" Mom asks. "I hear the search party was out pretty late. She might even still have some people looking for her."

"She walked up the driveway as we were getting ready to come in," I say.

My parents exchange a look, and I hope to god that means they didn't see us kissing.

"Is she okay?" Dad asks.

"Looks like it," I say, searching her for visible bite marks or scratches. "I guess the neighborhood cats know not to mess with her."

"She's a celebrity. They know their place." Mom shrugs. "But we can take her to the vet tomorrow, just to be sure everything checks out."

"You're a bad girl, and I'm so happy to see you," I say, smacking a big kiss on Selma's head before she successfully leaps out of my arms and tears off down the hallway toward my room.

"By the way, Mom, this is Duke. He and Dad already met."

"Oh, I've heard quite a bit about you from Terrell, Duke," Mom says with a sly smile. "Nice to meet you."

Duke shakes her hand and says the same while I try not to melt from embarrassment.

"Looks like we won't know the election results until late," Mom says, smoothing my braids. "How are you feeling about it?"

"Nervous, mostly. But . . . I guess it helps to know I did all I could."

"You've done more than most people would ever dream of, sweetie. Not a lot of people stay this committed to a cause. No matter how this turns out, we're proud of you."

"So proud," Dad says, giving me a fist bump. "And tired. We're going to watch the results from bed. Don't stay up too late. You have *school* tomorrow, remember?"

"Good night," I say, watching them walk down the hall to their bedroom.

I'm too nervous and tired to eat, and Duke says the same. I fill Selma's bowls with fresh food and water, and post a picture of her online with a quick but heartfelt thank-you so everyone knows she's home.

Then we settle on the couch, our bodies finally giving in to the exhaustion of the day. I turn the TV to one of the millions of twenty-four-hour news channels providing nonstop election coverage. Their voices instantly give me a headache, so I turn the volume low and look at Duke.

"The votes are so close."

"We could still win," he says, taking my hand in his.

It's impossible to tell.

"I'm not expecting anything."

But I like the feeling of his fingers threaded between

mine. It makes me feel like we're in this together, win or lose.

"Listen, I get it if you just want to go back to . . . friends? Or whatever we were when we met this morning," he says, his eyes tracing the features of my face. "Today was . . . a lot."

"I don't want to go back to the way things were," I say, leaning my head against his shoulder. "But I might need to take things slow."

"Yeah, me too," he says with a smile. "Gonna be pinching myself tomorrow, wondering if I really met you."

"Let's document it." I pull out my phone.

His long arms hold it out for a selfie, and I know I must look like crap after the day we've just had, but I don't care. I'm happy. I lean into him, his free arm wrapped around me as he snaps a picture. And when we pull it up, we do look tired and a little disheveled, but I like it. It proves we made it through the day.

I set my phone aside and Duke leans in for a kiss. He runs his hands through my braids, and I notice he spends a lot of time sliding his finger and thumb over the hot-pink one. My favorite one. I hope I never forget the feeling of his lips meeting mine.

I hope I never forget this day.

Once again, an insistent meow interrupts us, and this time, Selma is sitting in front of the couch.

"So you run off all day, making thousands of people worry about you, and now you don't want to be ignored? Oh, Selma," I say, scooping her up and setting her on my lap.

She settles right down, content after a meal and fresh water, and starts grooming herself.

On the TV, the news anchor says it will be a while before the final results come in.

"Do you need to get home?" I ask Duke, scared he's going to say yes. I don't think I can go through this alone. Not after all we've been through.

"No way. I'm here till the end." He gently strokes Selma's back. "Even if things don't go our way, it'll be all right. We'll get through it."

"We kind of have to, huh?" I say.

"Yeah. And we got this, Marva. No matter what."

He's right.

We got this.

ACKNOWLEDGMENTS

I am grateful to so many people who helped bring Marva and Duke's story to the page.

Laura Schreiber! I have so much gratitude for your editorial prowess, encouragement, and humor. Working with you on this book was so much fun, and I'm thankful for your guidance and enthusiasm through every stage of the process. Eartha Kitty forever!

To Tina Dubois, my literary agent and dear friend, thank you for everything, always. You've been with me since the very beginning of this publishing journey, and I'm so proud of how far we've come.

To the team at Hyperion—Emily Meehan, Stephanie Owens Lurie, Dina Sherman, Melissa Lee, Danny Diaz, Marci Senders, Sara Liebling, Guy Cunningham, Marybeth Tregarthen, LaToya Maitland, Holly Nagel, Danielle DiMartino, Vicki Korlishin, Elena Blanco, Kim Knueppel, Sarah Sullivan, Kori Neal, Monique Diman, Lia Murphy, Michael Freeman, Molly Kong, and Sara Boncha—thank you for treating me and this book with such kindness and respect. It's been a joy and an honor to work with you all.

Stephanie Singleton, thank you for the beautiful cover art and for bringing my characters to life in exactly the way I pictured them.

Thank you to librarians, educators, and booksellers for supporting and sharing my work with young people, and to my readers for trusting me with the stories I tell.

Thank you to my parents for instilling in me the importance of voting from a young age, for encouraging me to educate myself on candidates and what their campaigns stand for, and for reminding me to always use my voice.

And, finally, thank you to all the activists and people who dedicated their lives to voting rights for the disenfranchised, particularly for Black people in the Southern United States, where my family hails from. This was difficult, dangerous work that was often met with extreme violence or other retaliation, yet they persisted through hardships that seem nearly unfathomable now. Their courage and determination will not be forgotten, and their legacy remains strong in the continuing fight for freedom and equality.